MW01681345

A CAGE PAINTED RED

The Stained Series

Jessica Nicholls

Copyright © 2026 Jessica Nicholls

The characters and events portrayed in this book are fictitious. Any similarity to real persons, living or dead, is coincidental and not intended by the author.

No part of this book may be reproduced, or stored in a retrieval system, or transmitted in any form or by any means, electronic, mechanical, photocopying, recording, or otherwise, without express written permission of the publisher.

ISBN Paperback: 978-0-473-78068-5

To the readers who hunger for the forbidden - who chase stories that crawl under your skin and refuse to let go. You don't want safe. You want the kind of words that make your pulse race and your breath catch, the kind that leave marks. Thank you for your fearlessness, your fire, and for craving exactly what I'm serving.

CONTENT WARNING

Let's be honest - you're here for the unhinged, the unfiltered, and the unapologetically dark. Expect: obsession disguised as devotion, dubious consent, violence that'll make you flinch and keep reading, psychological manipulation, explicit sexual content, and characters who wouldn't know a healthy relationship if it bit them.

If you made it past the dedication and the warnings, you already know what you're in for. ***Welcome to the cage.***

"Stone walls do not a prison make, nor iron bars a cage."

- RICHARD LOVELACE, TO ALTHEA, FROM PRISON.

CHAPTER 1

Freya

The sunlight came through the pines in long gold streaks, the kind that made the air look holy. The ten large rustic cabins lined the main path like teeth in a smile. Each cabin had four rooms with three sets of bunks to a room. The wood smelled of cedar and something sharp, something wrong.

The gardens were neat, the grass trimmed with military precision, and the river that cut through the center of the property was so clear it looked like poured glass. It babbled under the back fence and disappeared into the deep trees, a ribbon of blue that promised if you followed it, you might find the edge of the world. In the early morning, mist rose from the water like the breath of something sleeping beneath the surface.

I sat up, the rough wool blanket pooling at

my waist. The first thing I did, as I did every morning since I got here, was touch my throat. There, resting against my collarbone, was the silver necklace. A heavy, cool thing, the metal unblemished. A circle, etched with four sharp points reaching outward like a compass. Loyalty, Perfection, Worship, Truth.

Father Michael had pressed it into my palm on my third day, his face warm as a furnace door.

"You are found now, Freya," he had told me. "Let this guide you. North, South, East, West, there is no direction where we are not with you."

I traced the southern point, Perfection, with my thumb.

Before this place, there had been my mother's voice at three in the morning. Slurred and sharp, cutting through thin walls.

"You're nothing, Freya. Just like your father. Nothing."

I pressed the compass point harder into my thumb until the edge bit. Then I let it go.

I remembered my first morning here, waking to a full stomach for the first time in longer than I could count. I had cried. I didn't know why. I pressed my face into the blanket and let it happen, then went to prayer and smiled.

Inside the cabin, the other eleven girls were already moving. Pastel dresses, swept floors, plumped pillows. Ghosts performing tidiness. Outside, silence meant something was about to break. Here it was doctrine. It was part of the "freedom from the burdens of decision."

I slid out of my bunk and went to the small wardrobe near the door. Nothing here was mine, exactly. But the clothes were always clean, always whole, always there. No holes in the elbows. No mysterious stains from a mother who didn't care. I pulled on a pale blue dress and brushed my hair until it hung straight, checking my reflection in the small mirror bolted to the wall.

Appearances must be pristine. Smiles must be gentle. The dress felt crisp against my skin, smelling faintly of lavender from the communal laundry. Outside, I could hear the morning sounds of the compound: the creak of cabin doors opening in synchronized rhythm, the soft shuffle of feet on gravel paths, the distant clang of the kitchen preparing breakfast. Everything here moved like clockwork. Predictable. Safe. The two words I'd spent my whole life trying to find.

I practiced my smile in the glass. Soft. Unthreatening. Grateful. It wasn't entirely a lie. I remembered the scrape of carpet against my cheek, bottles against the wall, my mother's voice like broken glass. Compared to that, this was Eden.

Mealtimes were at seven, twelve and six. Baths were at seven in the evening. Chores were assigned on a weekly rotation. Father Michael called it 'becoming one with us all.' A bell chimed from the white-washed prayer hall, a single clear note that vibrated in the morning air. I stepped outside.

The morning was cold enough to see my breath, but not so cold that it bit. Dew clung to the grass like scattered glass. Somewhere in the distance, a bird called out, a sharp, lonely sound that was quickly swallowed by the silence.

Immediately, Valerie fell into step beside me. Mid-twenties. Pale skin, dark hair pulled into a severe bun. She had been here years. Whatever person she'd been before had been sanded smooth. There was nothing left to catch on, no edges, no shadow of whoever she'd once been. Just the smile, always the smile, serene and exact and utterly empty.

"Good morning, sister," Valerie whispered.

"Good morning," I replied.

We walked in pairs and were always watched. Two of Father Michael's enforcers stood by the garden fence, scanning the line. Same clothes as everyone else, white shirts, dark pants, but the stillness was different. Carved into them. Hands clasped. Eyes that moved without the rest of the face moving. Like statues. Like soldiers. Like something that had forgotten it used to be a man.

The one on the left was named Thomas. Young. Jaw like granite, eyes the colour of river stones, grey and cold and not quite there. I'd seen him smile once, during a communal meal when Father Michael told a joke. It hadn't reached his eyes.

The other enforcer was James, older, with

silver threading through his dark hair and a scar that ran from his left eyebrow to his cheek. He never smiled at all. As we passed, his gaze tracked our movement the way you track something you're deciding whether to kill. I kept my focus on the ground, my steps measured.

Thomas shifted his weight as we passed, and I heard the crunch of gravel beneath his boot. The sound was too loud in the morning quiet, and several girls flinched. He noticed; the corner of his mouth moved. Not a smile. Something that fed on the flinching.

"Eyes forward," he said, his tone low and smooth. "Father Michael is waiting."

We passed the river. I glanced at the water, watching it rush under the back fence, and thought of wardrobes, fur coats, snow. A lion that spoke. I had read that book so many times the spine had split. Lucy stepped through and found a whole world on the other side, wild and cold and alive.

This place was my Narnia.

I almost believed it.

The birds stopped singing. It happened near the perimeter, a sudden absence of sound as we approached the prayer hall. The woods beyond the fence pressed closer, the shadows between the trees deeper than they should have been. Something held its breath. I felt the back of my neck prickle.

I looked ahead, past the garden beds bursting

with tomatoes and corn, to the large house at the very top of the hill. Father Michael's house. The only building with a door that remained locked. We girls were not permitted on the porch. The windows were always draped with heavy white cloth. It was the forbidden core of their family, the place where the elders gathered, where Father Michael retreated for his rest.

As I watched, the front door opened.

A girl stepped out.

Sarah. Cabin Two. Summoned for private prayer three days ago. Three days. I hadn't seen her at meals, hadn't seen her at evening baths, hadn't seen her anywhere.

And now here she was.

Sarah stood on the porch for a moment, blinking in the sunlight. Her dress ironed to perfection, her hair smooth and gleaming. She moved like a marionette. Her hands hung at her sides, fingers slightly curled. When she took a step down from the porch it was mechanical. Precise. Off.

But it was her eyes.

Sarah used to sneak grins during silent meditation. Eyes bright, always on the edge of laughing at something private. The kind of person who held onto herself even here.

Now her eyes were different. Not serene. Not filled with the holy light Father Michael preached. Empty, a blank that wasn't peace, that wasn't anything, like someone had reached inside and scooped out everything that made Sarah, Sarah. She walked past me and Valerie without looking up, a smile on her face like something practiced in a mirror until the muscles remembered without the mind.

My stomach dropped.

"Sarah?" I whispered, the word escaping before I could stop it.

She didn't respond. Didn't even acknowledge that I'd spoken. She just kept walking, her steps measured and even, heading toward the prayer hall.

Valerie nudged my arm. Her fingers were cold where they touched my skin. When I looked at her, I saw something flicker in her eyes. Fear? Warning? Gone too quickly to tell.

"Face forward, Freya," Valerie murmured, her voice thinned. "Focus on Truth."

I swallowed hard. I looked down at the compass around my neck. Truth.

I wanted to believe this was home. I wanted to believe the safety of the full belly and the clean clothes were worth Sarah's eyes. Worth the way Thomas had watched us flinch and been pleased by it.

But as we walked into the shadow of the prayer hall, the heavy wooden doors groaning open to swallow us whole, I felt the chain around my neck press into my skin.

I straightened my spine, pasted the gentle smile onto my face, and stepped inside.

The wood smelled of cedar and something sharp and wrong.

CHAPTER 2

Andre

Dawn patrol was my favourite duty.

The compound in the early hours belonged to the faithful and the watchful, those who had earned the right to witness the family's awakening. I walked the perimeter in silence, my boots finding purchase on the gravel without disturbing the morning quiet. The fence line was my domain. Every post, every gap, every point of vulnerability memorised and catalogued.

This was holy work.

The fence kept the poison out. Kept the family safe. I took pride in the precision, the discipline, the absolute control we maintained here. Nothing entered these gates without Father Michael's blessing. Nothing left without his permission.

I paused at the eastern gate, checking the

lock. Secure. As it should be. As it always was when I was on duty.

The river babbled beyond the back fence, indifferent to our order. I watched it for a moment, the way it churned and frothed where it slipped under the chain-link. That gap bothered me. Water couldn't be contained, couldn't be controlled. It was chaos made liquid, and it ran right under our wall every single morning like it was laughing at us.

But Father Michael said even the river served our purpose. "Let it flow, Andre," he'd told me once, his hand resting on my shoulder, warm and certain. "It reminds us of what we've escaped. The wild current of the world beyond these walls."

I believed him. I believed everything he said.

My mother slept peacefully in her cabin. She'd been here fifteen years now. Fifteen years of safety, of purpose, of being valued instead of used. Before the compound she had been a woman the world consumed slowly, like something left out in the weather. I had been a boy who watched it happen and couldn't stop it.

Father Michael had stopped it.

That was what I protected. That was why I walked this fence every morning before the sun fully rose, checking every post, every lock, every place where the outside world pressed against ours.

The bell chimed from the prayer hall, a single

pure note that cut through the morning air.

Time for assembly.

I took my position at the back of the hall. The shadow at the compound's spine. Girls filed in, paired and silent, their dresses rustling. I knew every face. Every behavioural pattern. It was my job to spot the fractures before they spread.

Father Michael says doubt is contagious.

I am the quarantine.

The new girl entered with Valerie.

I'd been briefed on her arrival three days ago. Freya. Twenty-four, maybe twenty-five. Runaway from an abusive home. Found at a bus station with nothing but a backpack and desperation. Standard recruit profile.

My assessment began automatically.

Age: Young. Still formable.

Build: Thin, malnourished. Recent trauma carried in the shoulders, the way she held her arms close to her body.

Behaviour: Trying too hard to blend in. Overcompensating.

Eyes: Too alert. Scanning. Calculating, even while she performed submission.

She touched the necklace repeatedly. A nervous habit, not reverence. She bit her lip when she concentrated, a tell that said she was thinking too much instead of simply accepting. The southern compass point, Perfection, pressed under her thumb over and over, the way you worry a loose thread without realising you're unravelling something.

She was afraid, but not of the right things. She feared discovery, not damnation.

I watched her settle onto the kneeling cushion, watched the way her hands shook slightly as she folded them in her lap. New converts were always nervous. I'd seen dozens of them, that particular combination of relief and residual terror, the body still braced for a blow that didn't come.

But there was something different about this one.

She looked up for just a second, her gaze sweeping the hall, and our eyes met across the distance. A fraction of a moment. Long enough for me to see the intelligence burning there, the stubborn will she was trying very hard to bury under downcast eyes and careful hands.

Then she looked away. Her cheeks flushed.

I should have looked away too. Should have continued my scan of the room, logging the other girls, checking for other fractures. That was protocol. That was the job.

My gaze stayed on her.

Professional interest, I told myself. *She's a flight risk. I need to assess the threat level.*

I noted the curve of her neck. The way her pulse jumped visibly in her throat when Father Michael's voice lifted. The slight tremor in her hands, there then gone, controlled but not extinguished. I noted the exact angle she tipped her chin when Valerie murmured something to her, that small sideways tilt that meant she was listening but not agreeing. I noted all of it.

I did not reach for my notebook.

I scanned the rest of the room. Third row left, Mary, still showing signs of grief, would need additional conditioning. Front row, Rebecca, flawless posture, perfect compliance. A model convert. I moved my eyes over them all with the same systematic attention I gave the fence line every morning.

Then they drifted back.

Freya was mouthing the words of the opening prayer, but she wasn't saying them. I could tell from the way her lips moved; she was mimicking, not believing. Performing, not participating.

She was lying. Lying to every person in this room, to Father Michael himself, with her folded hands and her downcast eyes and her pale blue dress. She was a small, deliberate act of defiance wearing the costume of compliance.

It should have disgusted me.

I noted the exact shade of her hair in the morning light that came through the high windows. The way the necklace sat against her collarbone, rising and falling with each breath.

This is the chaos Father Michael warns about, I told myself.

I believed that too.

I just didn't look away.

CHAPTER 3

Freya

The bell rang at twilight, a single clear note that vibrated through the floorboards of our cabin.

"Get dressed," Valerie said, unfolding from her knees where she'd been praying. Her voice was soft, unhurried, the way every voice here was soft and unhurried. "It is the Welcoming. We must bear witness."

I looked down at the silver compass on my chest. Loyalty. Perfection. Worship. Truth. The metal was cool against my skin. For the first time since I'd arrived, the heavy ache in my chest, the one born of a childhood spent screaming and hiding, seemed to loosen its grip, just a fraction. I straightened my spine and told myself that was a good thing.

"What is the Welcoming?" I asked, smoothing the fabric of my pale dress, anxious to look right. "Is it a ceremony?"

"The family grows today," Valerie said, her eyes already distant, her face smoothed to that particular blankness I was learning to imitate. "A new lamb has come to the fold. We must be present to welcome her into the peace."

I followed her out of the cabin and joined the stream of women flowing from all ten cabins at once. We walked in pairs, silent, our dresses rustling in the evening breeze. Nobody spoke. Nobody looked around. They moved with a synchronized precision that reminded me of birds in formation, beautiful and deeply strange, and I tried to match their pace, their posture, the particular quality of their stillness.

The sun was dipping below the tree line, painting the compound in long shadows of purple and bruised orange. The river glinted like a blade in the fading light.

It looked like a postcard for paradise.

The air changed as we approached the prayer hall. It grew heavy, thick with beeswax and something sharper underneath, something that tingled at the back of my throat and coated my tongue with sweetness. Incense, maybe. Or something else. The double doors were thrown wide, spilling gold light out onto the grass, and I stepped inside and took my place beside Valerie on the hard wooden bench and sat up very straight and told myself I was home.

"Who is it?" I whispered. "The new girl?"

"Elara," Valerie whispered back, not looking at me. Her eyes were fixed on the front of the room, shining with a fervent light that made me feel like an outsider looking through glass. "She came from the city. She is troubled. She doesn't understand the gift yet."

Before I could ask what that meant, the chanting began.

It wasn't a song. It was a low, rhythmic drone that seemed to come from the floorboards themselves, from the walls, from the air. *One with us all. One with us all.* I closed my eyes and let it move through me. The individual voices melded into something larger than themselves, a collective pulse that pressed against the inside of my ribs. It blocked out everything: the smell of my mother's apartment, the cold linoleum of the bathroom floor where I used to sleep when she brought men home, the particular silence before a door opened that I'd learned to dread.

Here there was only the rhythm. Only us.

I found myself swaying slightly, my lips forming the words.

Then the double doors at the back of the hall opened.

Two enforcers walked in, supporting a girl between them.

She was young, maybe nineteen. She wore the plain white shift of a novice, already stained with dirt and tears. Her hair was a tangled blonde mess, her eyes wide and rimmed with red, her knuckles white where she gripped the arms of the men holding her. She was screaming, a high thin sound that cut through the chanting like a blade.

"Let me go! I want to go home! My dad is looking for me! You can't do this!"

I flinched. My hands gripped the edge of the bench.

Something in her voice went through me before I could stop it, something that remembered what it felt like to be that terrified, to scream into a room where no one was going to help you. I shoved it down hard. I looked around at the women on either side of me, their faces serene and unchanged, and I made my face do the same.

Couldn't she see how clean it was here? How safe?

The enforcers brought her to the center of the room and forced her to her knees. She thrashed, clawing at their arms, kicking out.

"Silence," a voice said.

The chanting stopped. The silence rushed back in, thick and absolute.

Father Michael descended from his raised platform. He moved with a slow fluid grace, his white robes sweeping the floor, catching the candlelight until he seemed to glow. He didn't look angry. He looked like a parent approaching a child with a skinned knee; patient, loving, certain that he already knew how this ended.

He stopped in front of her.

She froze, looking up at him, her chest heaving.

"Elara," he said, his voice a warm roll of sound that seemed to fill every corner of the room at once. "You are safe now. The world cannot hurt you here."

"You're a monster," she sobbed. "You kidnapped me."

"I saved you," he corrected, gently.

He reached out and touched her forehead. I leaned forward without meaning to.

His palm settled against her skin, and the change was instant.

Her eyes fluttered. The screaming stopped, cut off as if someone had unplugged it. She didn't collapse; she just settled. The tension drained from her shoulders, her jaw unclenched, her fists unfurled. The terror dissolved from her face and what replaced it looked, from where I sat, remarkably like relief. Like the moment you put down something you've been carrying for so long you forgot it wasn't part of your body.

It looked like surrender.

"You will become one with us all," Father Michael said, beginning his slow circle around her. "You will become one with us all." Each pass, a touch: her shoulder, her hand, the back of her neck. I watched her breathing slow. I watched her eyes stop moving and settle on him, steady and soft and utterly still.

"Rise, Elara," he said.

She stood without hesitation. No stumbling, no confusion. She looked at him with an expression that was almost holy.

"Thank you, Father," she said.

"Go to your sisters. Wash. Eat. Be at peace."

She turned and walked back down the aisle. As she passed our row I looked for the girl who had been screaming. I couldn't find her. The girl who passed me was serene. Beautiful, even. Whatever Father Michael had done had smoothed her flat.

I turned to Valerie. "She seems much better," I whispered.

Valerie squeezed the girl's hand as she passed. The girl smiled back, a perfect serene curve.

"Welcome, sister," Valerie whispered.

I sat back. The tension in my own chest had unknotted somewhere during the ceremony without my noticing. I looked down at the silver compass. The four points caught the candlelight.

I was safe here.

I closed my eyes and let the resumed prayer wash over me, and I made a choice: I buried the small cold prickle at the back of my neck. Buried the part of me that had recognized the terror in Elara's voice. Buried the thought forming just below the surface, quiet and terrible, that the blankness in her eyes wasn't peace.

That it was absence.

That what I'd just watched wasn't healing.

I was good at burying things. I'd had a lot of practice.

I was going to be fine here.

I pressed the compass point into my thumb until the edge bit, and smiled, and believed it.

CHAPTER 4

Freya

The garden work was supposed to be meditative.

Father Michael said so at every morning assembly, his voice rolling over us like warm water: *the earth does not lie, sisters. Put your hands in it and feel the truth.* So I knelt in the dirt between the rows of kale and tried to feel the truth, and what I felt was my knees aching and the sun too bright on the back of my neck and a low persistent hum under my skin that no amount of weeding seemed to quiet.

Pull the weed. Leave the good plant.

I pulled. I left. I tried to be grateful.

The woman working beside me, Margaret, had said "beautiful morning" and smiled her serene empty smile, and I had said "yes, beautiful" with my hands shaking and my teeth pressed together. She was humming now, a hymn I didn't recognise, soft and repetitive, the kind of melody that got inside your head and stayed there. I tried to catch the tune and couldn't. I tried to let it soothe me and couldn't do that either.

I glanced at the woman working two rows over. Hannah, I thought someone had called her. Older, maybe forty, grey threaded through her brown hair. Her hands moved with the same steady rhythm as everyone else's, but there was a tightness around her eyes. A set to her jaw that looked like someone trying very hard not to think. She looked up suddenly, caught me staring, and something flashed across her face before she looked away. Recognition, maybe. Warning.

Then the birds stopped.

One moment the forest was alive with sound. The next, silence dropped over the tree line like a hand pressed over a mouth. Not peaceful. Wrong. The particular quality of silence I had learned to read as a child, the gathering, the held breath, the moment before.

My hands froze mid-pull.

I didn't look up. I kept my eyes on the dirt, kept my hands moving, but my skin had gone electric. Through my peripheral vision I caught them: two figures moving along the fence line in precise synchronisation, hands clasped behind their backs, heads turning in slow arcs. Not Thomas or James. These were different enforcers, harder somehow, their movements too controlled, like men who had been trained to the point where training replaced instinct entirely.

One of them stopped. Directly across from where I knelt.

I could feel his gaze on me the way you feel a hand hovering just above your skin without touching it. My heart hammered. I kept my hands moving, kept my breathing steady, kept my eyes down.

Pull the weed. Leave the good plant. I am good. I am here to stay.

The creak of leather from his belt or his boots, I couldn't tell which. The sound went through me like a current, dragged up a memory I'd spent years burying: my stepfather's boots on the floorboards going quiet outside my bedroom door. The particular silence of a man deciding. My body didn't know the difference between then and now. It just knew the leather, the stillness, the waiting.

My hands were trembling when I reached for the next weed.

After an eternity, his boots crunched on gravel again. Moving on.

The breath I'd been holding came out slow and silent.

Animals go quiet when predators are near, I thought. *There are no predators here. Only family.*

But if we were family, why did we need a fence? If this was paradise, why did it need guards?

I pushed the thought down before it could

finish forming. A few yards away, two younger girls from Cabin One moved in tandem toward the river, their matching braids swaying in perfect rhythm, their faces soft and unfocused. The elders called it unity. I watched them and felt something cold settle in my stomach that I didn't have a name for yet.

The robin came back first. Then a jay, a crow, the normal soundtrack resuming as if someone had pressed play on a recording. The forest exhaled.

Margaret smiled at the sky. "Beautiful morning," she said again, softly.

"Yes," I agreed. "Beautiful."

* * * *

By the time the sun dipped below the tree line the exhaustion in my body was deep and honest, the kind that usually meant dreamless sleep. We ate, prayed, bathed, marched back in the dark. The other girls were asleep within minutes, their breathing soft and rhythmic, and I lay on my bunk staring at the ceiling beams and waited for sleep that didn't come.

I touched the necklace. The metal was warm from my skin, the four points pressing into my fingertips. Loyalty. Perfection. Worship. Truth.

My mind kept snagging on the gap.

It had been late when the van brought me in. I remembered the gates opening, headlights cutting through dark. I remembered Thomas's kind smile, his hand gentle on my elbow as he guided me toward, and then nothing. The dining hall? No, it was too late for dinner. My cabin? But I had no memory of that first night. No memory of meeting my bunkmates, of unpacking, of being shown where to sleep.

The next clear memory was breakfast. Eggs, toast, the silver necklace already warm against my skin as if it had been there for hours.

Twelve hours. Gone.

You were exhausted, I told myself. *Traumatised. People don't remember everything.*

The rationalisation felt like pressing a thumb over a crack in a dam.

I could feel the shape of the missing time, its weight and texture, the way you can feel a word sitting just behind your tongue without being able to say it. Something had happened in those twelve hours. Something I was not supposed to remember.

I closed my eyes and told myself to sleep.

The darkness behind my eyelids began to strobe.

Flash.

I was standing. My legs barely held me. The air smelled antiseptic, sterile, nothing like the pine and earth of the compound.

Flash.

A light, blindingly white. Not the warm yellow of morning; clinical, electric, the kind that left afterimages burned into the retina. I couldn't see the room. Only the white, drilling into my skull. I tried to lift my hands to cover my eyes and couldn't. My arms hung at my sides like they belonged to someone else.

"It's alright, child."

Father Michael's voice, close and resonant, vibrating in my chest rather than reaching my ears through air.

His hand cupped the back of my neck. Dry and hot and absolute. It didn't hurt. It was worse than hurt; it was a grip that said I have you in a language older than words, and my body understood it completely.

"You are empty," the voice said, soothing and terrible. "The world filled you with poison. With chaos."

Flash.

The light intensified. Tears tracked down my cheeks but my eyelids wouldn't close. I was trapped in the brightness, drowning in it. Images flickered at the edges: my mother's face. Breaking glass. Cigarettes and cheap vodka. The feeling of being small and powerless and invisible.

"We must make you clean. You will become one with us all."

The phrase landed differently here than it had in the prayer hall. In the prayer hall it had been a tide pulling at my ankles, seductive, almost warm. Here it was a hand reaching into my chest. I felt it move down my spine and settle into my bones like something taking up residence. Like it was rewriting something fundamental, some central column of selfhood, replacing it with hollow space.

"You will become one with us all."

My memories flickered and thinned. The paperback with the cracked spine. The smell of my childhood bedroom. The feel of carpet against my cheek. Each one loosening, pulling away from me, scoured off like sandcastles surrendering to a tide.

"You will become one with us all."

And somewhere underneath the terror was the thing I couldn't forgive myself for feeling: relief. Because if I wasn't Freya anymore, I didn't have to carry her. Her pain, her shame, every humiliation and cold night and door that had closed against her. I could just dissolve.

I could just stop.

I gasped, my body jackknifing upright in the bunk.

The cabin rushed back in. Pine and darkness and Valerie's soft snores and the cool draft from the window. I clamped my hand over my mouth and pressed until the sob couldn't get out, my breath coming in short ragged bursts.

Slowly, I reached for my throat.

The necklace was there. The four points dug into my fingers. But the heat of his palm hadn't faded. I could still feel the ghost of it at the back of my neck, warm and possessive, and I didn't know if what I'd just experienced was a dream or a memory and that not-knowing was the most frightening thing of all.

I am one with them, my mind offered, quiet and unbidden, like a thing that had been waiting.

I pressed the southern point, Perfection, into my thumb until my skin split around it.

I am not, I thought back. *I am not. I am Freya. I am still here.*

I lay back down and kept my eyes open and my hand on the necklace, and I waited for the grey light of dawn to come and prove it.

CHAPTER 5

Freya

The river gap was exactly where I remembered it.

I had told myself I was drifting toward the eastern perimeter by accident, that my feet had found the riverbank without my permission while my hands were busy pulling weeds. But my hands had stopped moving three minutes ago and I was still standing here, staring at the place where the chain-link fence met the water and didn't quite reach the bottom.

The current churned against the posts, slapping at the mud where they sank into the bank. The gap was dark and narrow, maybe eighteen inches of rushing water between the bottom wire and the riverbed. I watched a dead leaf sweep into it and vanish instantly into the centre flow.

I could fit through there.

The thought arrived fully formed, sharp as a knife cut. Not a question. A fact.

I took a step back. My heart hammered.

Why would you do that? I asked myself. *To drown? To be swept away into nothing?*

I just need to know the layout, I reasoned, digging my nails into my palms until the sting cleared my head. *If I know the perimeter, I know where I'm safe. I know where the boundaries are.*

It was a lie. A pretty, flimsy lie, and I knew it the moment I told it. I wasn't memorising boundaries. I wasn't assessing safety. I was standing at a gap in the fence and my body was already calculating whether it could fit.

I turned away before I could finish the calculation.

But I didn't stop thinking about it.

****

Over the following weeks, the itch became unbearable.

It wasn't one thing. It was everything at once, a low persistent static under my skin that the routine couldn't touch. I woke before the bell and lay rigid in my bunk, listening to the other girls breathe. I moved through prayers and meals and chores with my face arranged correctly, smile soft, eyes down, hands folded, while something inside me vibrated at a frequency I couldn't name and couldn't quiet.

I stole again. Small things. A coin from the blessing jar. A safety pin from the laundry room.

A stub of pencil I found in the garden bed. I pressed them against my skin, cold and real, hidden in the fold of my bra. I didn't know what I was saving them for. I only knew they were mine, and that mattering felt like oxygen.

I started sleeping badly. The nightmares came every night without fail, fragments of white rooms and clinical light, Father Michael's hand at the back of my neck, the phrase drilling into me like something with teeth. I'd wake with my hands clawing the sheets and my throat raw, and I'd lie there in the dark pressing the compass point into my thumb and telling myself: *still here. Still me.*

Valerie noticed. Of course she did.

"You seem troubled, sister," she said one evening, folding her hands in that particular way that meant she was about to say something she considered a gift.

"I'm fine," I said.

"You should pray more," she said. "Prayer brings peace."

I looked at her face, smooth and certain, and I thought: the chanting is digging into my brain like worms. I thought: you are a woman who has forgotten she had edges. I thought: I would rather feel this terrible itch for the rest of my life than become whatever it is you've become.

I nodded. I smiled. "You're right," I said. "Thank you."

* * * *

The morning it broke open, the prayer hall smelled of beeswax and something beneath it, something sweet and slightly chemical that coated the back of my throat. I took my place on the floorboards in the long rows of women, knees on cold wood, hands folded, head bowed.

The murmuring began.

"Thank you for our bounty. Thank you for our purpose. We are small. We are one. We will be one with us all."

I moved my lips. The sounds died in my throat. The exhaustion from weeks of broken sleep pressed down on my shoulders like a physical weight, and underneath the weight was the vibration, always the vibration, and underneath that was a memory I hadn't summoned: a worn paperback cover with a lion on it.

Wild, untamed magic that broke wardrobes and melted winter. Magic that wasn't about rules or cleanliness or obedience. Magic that meant *you could leave.*

For a heartbeat the drone of the prayer hall faded entirely. In the silence of my own mind I wasn't Freya the compliant, Freya the grateful, Freya who kept her eyes down and her smile gentle. I was a girl stepping through a fur coat into a world where lions spoke and trees danced and no one could make you become one with anything.

I forgot to pray. I forgot to bow. I forgot to move my lips.

I just knelt there, staring at the knot in the

wood floor, and for one perfect suspended moment I was somewhere else entirely.

The silence didn't happen gradually. It was severed.

Forty voices cut off as if a switch had been thrown. The air pressurised instantly, dangerous, a held breath the size of the room.

I blinked. The other world evaporated. I was sitting straight while every other body in the hall bowed low.

Panic spiked through me, cold and electric. I started to drop, to correct, to become invisible again.

Too late.

"Freya."

Father Michael's voice. Not a shout; a soft, terrible purr that carried effortlessly across every inch of the room. The kind of voice that didn't need to raise itself because it had never in its life been ignored.

Slowly, I lifted my head.

His gaze locked onto mine from the dais. He didn't look angry. He looked the way you look at a broken cup; disappointed, patient, already knowing what came next.

"Come," he said.

The enforcers took my arms with that particular grip, firm and gentle and absolute, and walked me to the front of the hall. The walk felt endless. Forty pairs of eyes tracked me without any head lifting, their attention a pressure I could feel on my skin. I wondered if it was judgment. Then I thought: no. It's relief. Relief that it's me and not them.

They forced me to my knees at the base of the dais.

"Posture of Penitence," an enforcer murmured.

I pulled my arms behind my back, locked my hands at the base of my spine, spread my knees wide, lowered my chin. The floorboards bit into my kneecaps immediately. Within minutes my thighs were shaking, my shoulders screaming at the unnatural angle, sweat prickling on my forehead.

"Continue," Father Michael said to the room.

The chanting resumed. And now I was the lesson.

He began to speak. The disease of the self. The poison of distraction. Girls who believed their individual thoughts mattered more than the collective peace.

"The self is a cancer," he said, his voice melodic and patient. "It grows and spreads and consumes until there is nothing left but rot. We must cut it out. We must cleanse it. We must become one."

Then the phrase.

"You will become one with us all."

It landed in my body differently now. Not the tide it had been in the Welcoming ceremony, pulling warmly at my ankles. Not even the hand reaching into my chest from the nightmare. This was a chisel. Driven into the exact place where I still lived, where the itch and the stolen coins and the gap in the fence all lived, the small fierce core of me that had survived my mother and the cold and the apartment floor and every door that had ever closed against me.

"You will become one with us all."

My vision blurred with tears I refused to let fall. The pain was blinding, a white-hot fire in my knees and thighs and shoulders, demanding everything, leaving no room for thought.

But it left room for one thing.

I looked up at the rows of women. Valerie, second row, face serene, lips moving, eyes closed. Not looking at me. Not concerned. As natural as the sunrise.

They weren't my friends. They weren't my sisters. They were hostages who had fallen in love with their chains. Here, suffering wasn't an accident; it was a tool, a file used to sand down the rough edges of a person until they fit seamlessly into the machine. Individuality wasn't just a flaw here. It was a crime.

I looked at the white-washed walls, the neat garden beds visible through the open doors.

This wasn't salvation. This was a cage with flowers painted on the bars.

The clean dresses, the full bellies, the safety — they were velvet wrapped around iron shackles, and I had been so hungry, so cold, so desperate for warmth that I had let them close around my wrists and called it home.

Father Michael looked down at me. His eyes expected defeat. Expected the light to drain out until I was just another empty vessel, ready to be filled.

I gritted my teeth until my jaw ached.

I thought of the lion. I thought of the wardrobe. I thought of the girl who had survived a chaotic, terrifying world on thirty-seven dollars and a battered paperback and nothing else, because she had fire in her gut that nobody had managed to put out yet.

I held onto the pain. I let it be mine.

I am not one with you, I thought, the words a stone in the centre of my chest, small and hard and completely immovable. *I am Freya. I am still here.*

I stared back at Father Michael through the blur of tears and I swore, quietly and completely, that I would let every bone in my body break before I became what he was trying to make me.

His eyes narrowed. Just slightly. Just enough.

I smiled at him. A real one, small and private and entirely my own.

He looked away first.

CHAPTER 6

Andre

I stood in my usual position at the back of the prayer hall, hands clasped, expression neutral. To anyone watching I was the perfect enforcer; present, vigilant, carved from the same stone as the walls.

I had not moved when Freya drifted away from the chant.

I should have. Protocol was clear; enforcers corrected minor infractions before they became major ones. I had watched her eyes drift toward some internal landscape I couldn't access, watched the exact moment the girls around her noticed and the ripple of disapproval moved through the congregation like a cold wind. I had watched all of it and stayed exactly where I was.

Curious.

The word sat in my chest like a splinter. I was not supposed to be curious about the girls here. I was supposed to assess, report, contain. Instead I had watched her inhabit her private rebellion and wanted to know what was inside it.

Now she was kneeling at the front of the hall, arms wrenched behind her back, knees grinding into floorboards, and it was my fault.

"You will become one with us all."

Father Michael's voice filled the room, rhythmic and absolute. I had heard those words a thousand times. Spoken them myself during retrievals. They were necessary. They were the cure for the disease of selfhood.

So why did they sound different today?

I watched her body shake with the strain of holding the position. An hour had passed, maybe more. Time moved strangely in the prayer hall during corrections. Her thighs trembled, the muscles failing in increments. Sweat darkened the collar of her dress. Her hands, locked at the base of her spine, had lost their colour entirely.

My hands clenched at my sides. Automatic. Unconscious.

I forced them open.

I had stood in this exact spot during dozens of corrections. Watched girls held in the Posture until they wept and begged and promised to be better. Watched Father Michael's patient, gentle conditioning break spirit after spirit. I had felt nothing but professional satisfaction each time. Another soul brought back from the edge. Another vessel prepared.

Why was this different?

She was just another girl who believed her individual thoughts mattered more than the collective peace. She would learn, or she would leave. Simple. Clean. Ordained.

I imagined crossing the hall. Pulling her to her feet. Telling Father Michael the lesson had been learned, that further correction was unnecessary.

The fantasy was so vivid I could feel her weight against me.

What the hell are you thinking?

Father Michael circled her like a predator assessing wounded prey, his voice never wavering, his patience infinite, because he already knew how this ended. He always knew how it ended.

"The self is a cancer," he said, his voice melodic and unhurried. "It grows and spreads and consumes until there is nothing left but rot. We must cut it out. We must cleanse it. We must become one."

Then his eyes found her face.

Then he stopped circling.

She was looking back at him.

Her body was failing, thighs shaking violently, tears streaming freely down her face, but her eyes were alive in a way that made everything else in the room seem dim by comparison. Not the glazed surrender I was used to. Not the frantic bargaining of girls who wanted the pain to stop. Something else entirely. A core of absolute stillness inside the trembling, watching him back with an attention that was almost scientific.

She smiled at him.

No. Don't do that. Don't provoke him.

Every enforcer instinct I had screamed to cross the floor, force her head down, make her submit before Father Michael decided the Posture wasn't sufficient. But I stood frozen, watching that terrible, beautiful smile, and the thought arrived before I could stop it.

She's magnificent.

It hit me like a physical blow. I buried it instantly, drove it down under layers of doctrine and duty and years of conditioning.

This was necessary. She was sick. This was the cure.

Father Michael's jaw tightened, just fractionally, the only crack in his serenity. Then he turned away from her. Dismissing her as if she were beneath his notice.

"Continue," he said to the congregation.

The chanting resumed. The assembly carried on as if nothing had happened. But Freya remained at the front, still in the Posture, the defiant smile still at the corners of her mouth even as fresh tears streaked her face. Father Michael knew he hadn't won. The knowledge of it sat in the set of his shoulders as he returned to the dais.

Inside my chest, something cracked open that I didn't know how to close.

****

When the last girl had filed out, Father Michael released her.

"You may go."

She tried to stand. Her legs buckled on the first attempt, the second, the third. Each time she caught herself on shaking arms and tried again. She swayed dangerously when she finally made it upright. But she didn't look at the enforcers. Didn't wait to be helped.

She walked out on her own broken legs.

I followed at a distance, maintaining the professional fiction that I was doing my job.

She went to Cabin Four. I expected her to collapse on her bunk. Instead she stood in the centre of the room for a long moment, just breathing, and then moved with a sudden purpose that made the hairs on the back of my neck rise. I positioned myself in the shadows outside the window. The curtains were thin.

Her hands shook as she opened the wardrobe. She didn't take anything from it. She reached under her mattress instead.

The book. That children's fantasy about wardrobes and magic she'd been reading by the light of the moon. I'd noted it weeks ago and flagged it as low-risk. A comfort object. Harmless.

She wrapped it in plastic, along with something else. Paper. Folded. Money?

She had been stealing.

The package went under her dress, against her stomach. Then her hands went to her neck.

The necklace.

She worked the clasp for a long time, her fingers fumbling, shaking too badly to manage the mechanism. The frustration built visibly in her face. Then it came loose.

She held the silver compass in her palm, staring at the four points. Loyalty. Perfection. Worship. Truth. She looked at them the way you look at something that was never really yours.

Then she set it on her pillow and walked out.

The certainty landed in my gut like a stone.

She wasn't going to wait. Wasn't going to plan, rest, recover. She was running right now, while her body was still broken from the punishment, while she could barely walk. The gap in the eastern fence. The river.

She would drown.

I should have raised the alarm. Should have called pursuit. Standard protocol for a runner was immediate response, all available enforcers, cut her off before the fence line.

I went to my quarters instead. Sat on the edge of my bunk. Stared at the wall while the minutes moved.

Each minute was another yard she gained.

I found myself hoping she made it. Hoping she found the gap, slipped through, let the river carry her somewhere beyond our walls and beyond my reach. Because if she succeeded, I wouldn't have to be the one to bring her back. Wouldn't have to be the one to deliver her to the white room. Wouldn't have to watch the light go out of those eyes.

But she wouldn't succeed. I was too good at my job. I knew every exit, every vulnerability, every pattern a runner followed in the dark.

My phone buzzed. A text from Father Michael.

Come to my office.

* * * *

He was sitting behind his desk, hands folded, expression the same serene mask he wore for every occasion.

"Sit, Andre."

I sat.

"You look tired," he said. Not a reprimand. Concerned. "How long has it been since you slept properly? Ate a real meal?" He tilted his head. "I ask because I care about you. Because I can see you carrying something you shouldn't have to carry alone."

I said nothing.

"She's gotten to you," he said, gently. Not an accusation. A diagnosis.

"She's a flight risk. I've been monitoring—"

"I know what you've been doing." His smile didn't shift. "I also know what you've been feeling. You're human, Andre. Humans develop fascinations with things that resist them. It's natural. It's also dangerous."

He stood, walked around the desk, placed a hand on my shoulder.

"Your mother is safe here. Has been safe for years. That safety isn't abstract; it requires maintaining the structures that make this family possible." His grip tightened, just slightly. "If you cannot maintain clarity with this girl, I would worry about your judgement. And if your judgement is compromised, then your usefulness to this family becomes uncertain."

The threat was warm. Loving, almost.

"I understand, Father."

"I knew you would." He released my shoulder, returning to his seat. "When she runs, and she will run, you will bring her back immediately. For intensive reintegration. The kind that leaves no room for defiance."

The white room. The chair. The lights.

"Yes, Father."

"You may go." A pause. "Andre. I trust you completely. You are my most faithful servant. Don't make me reconsider that."

"Never, Father."

****

I walked back through the compound on autopilot. The evening bell rang. Girls filed toward the dining hall in their synchronized pairs. The space where Freya should have been was an absence I felt before I looked for it.

In my quarters I lay on my bunk and stared at the ceiling and did not sleep.

I thought about the way she'd looked at Father Michael. The smile that had cost her so much and that she'd given anyway. The compass left on the pillow like a shed skin, like proof that she knew exactly what it represented and had decided it wasn't hers anymore.

Father Michael called her sick. Called her diseased. Called her something that needed to be fixed.

I had watched her walk out of that hall on legs that could barely hold her, and the only word that had come to me was the one I'd buried.

Magnificent.

Somewhere out in the dark she was moving toward the river, broken and furious and entirely, dangerously alive.

I was supposed to be the one who stopped that.

I lay in the dark and listened to the compound settle around me and wondered, for the first time in years, what exactly I was protecting.

CHAPTER 7

Freya

The resolve was a cold, hard stone in my gut as the prayer hall finally emptied.

My legs threatened to buckle with every step, my knees screaming from the hours on the floorboards, but I forced myself to move with the same rhythmic mechanical gait as the others. Head down. Hands folded. Just another girl walking back to her cabin. I was bruised and shaking and hollowed out, but I was awake, and being awake meant I could see.

I could see what this place really was beneath the scripture and the smiles.

Part of me, the part that remembered hunger and cold linoleum floors, wanted to stay. Wanted to believe that safety was worth the price. That obedience was a fair trade for a full belly and clean clothes and a bed that was always warm. But the larger part, the part that had survived on instinct and stubbornness and thirty-seven dollars and nothing else, knew better. This wasn't safety. It was just a different kind of trap.

I didn't plan it. There were no maps, no stolen keys, no conspiratorial whispers in the dark. It was simpler than that. It was a refusal. A decision made somewhere below the level of thought, in the part of me that Father Michael had been trying to reach for weeks and hadn't managed to touch.

I was leaving.

* * * *

The cabin was empty when I got there. The other girls were already at their assigned chores, scrubbing floors or hanging laundry in the thin morning light. I moved through the familiar space quickly, letting muscle memory carry me.

I opened the wardrobe. For a heartbeat I stood staring at the neat row of pastel dresses and thought about a soft grey cotton shirt with a fraying collar that smelled of home and vanilla. It was gone. Had been gone since I arrived. I mourned it, briefly and sharply, and then I let it go.

I reached under the mattress.

The Lion, the Witch and the Wardrobe. Dog-eared, spine cracked, pages soft with handling. My last real possession from before. I found the plastic wrapper the dresses had been packaged in when I arrived and wrapped the book tight with the money, sealing it against the water, and slipped the package under my dress against my stomach. Bulky and awkward, a hard lump against my ribs.

Then I reached behind my neck.

My fingers found the clasp and froze there. The metal was warm from my skin. I'd worn this compass every day since Father Michael had placed it around my neck; Loyalty, Perfection, Worship, Truth. For weeks those words had felt like shelter. Now they felt like a hand around my throat.

I tried to undo the clasp. My fingers fumbled, shaking too badly to manage the tiny mechanism. Once. Twice. Three times, sweat beading on my forehead, panic rising. What if I couldn't get it off? What if I was marked forever, branded as one of his girls even after I ran?

I closed my eyes. Forced myself to breathe. Pictured Lucy pushing through the fur coats into the dark, not knowing what was on the other side, going anyway.

The clasp gave.

The chain pooled in my palm. I looked at the four points one last time and then set the compass on my pillow; a white flag on a deserted battlefield. A gravestone for the girl I'd almost become.

I walked out of the cabin.

****

I didn't run. Running would mark me. I walked with my posture straight and my eyes forward, heading toward the garden beds, just another girl on another chore. Just part of the machine.

I passed Martha at the tomatoes. She looked up and our eyes met, and for a second the urge was so strong it almost moved my feet; grab her hand, whisper *come with me, we can go together, you don't have to stay here.* But Martha's eyes were already soft and unfocused, her smile already painted on. Whatever spark she'd arrived with was gone. Snuffed out quietly over weeks until there was nothing left to catch.

I couldn't save her. I could barely save myself.

I kept walking.

Footsteps behind me. Heavy. Measured. Male.

My blood went cold. I didn't stop. Didn't turn. Every muscle in my body pulled tight, ready.

"Freya." Thomas.

I turned slowly, keeping my face soft. "Yes, sir?"

He stood ten feet back, hands clasped, his river-stone eyes moving over me with the particular patience of a man who had caught liars before. "Where are you headed?"

"To gather herbs from the garden," I said. My voice didn't shake. I was almost proud of it. "For this evening's meal."

"The herb garden is in the opposite direction."

My heart stopped. Think. *Think.* "I wanted to check the wild mint by the river first. Valerie mentioned we were running low."

A long pause. His eyes narrowed fractionally, the calculation visible if you knew how to look. Then he nodded once. "Don't stray from the path."

"Yes, sir."

I waited until his boots rounded the corner of Cabin Two before I let myself breathe. My hands were shaking so badly I had to clasp them together.

Too close.

I slipped between the cabins and into the tree line, where the shadows were long and the ground was soft with pine needles, and I moved toward the sound of water.

****

The river looked gentle from the bank. It always had; that particular deception was part of the compound's aesthetic, the babbling water over smooth stones, the sunlight catching the surface. But I had watched it during chores, had clocked the way leaves got sucked into the eddies and didn't come back. I knew what was underneath the pretty surface.

I knew where the fence ended.

The gap was exactly where I remembered; a dark narrow slit where the current had eaten away at the bank, where the chain-link sagged and bent away from the riverbed. Maybe two feet of rushing water between wire and mud. I'd have to submerge completely.

I didn't let myself think about it. Thinking was how you talked yourself out of things.

I stepped off the bank.

The cold hit me like a fist driven straight into my sternum. Every muscle in my body seized at once, my lungs slamming shut, a scream locked behind my teeth that I could not let out, could not, because if I screamed they would hear me and it would be over. I stood chest-deep in the current with my mouth clamped shut and my eyes streaming and my whole body shaking so violently I could barely keep my feet.

Move. You have to move.

The rocks beneath my feet were slick with algae, treacherous, shifting. I tested each step before I trusted it, moving inches at a time while the current shoved at me from every direction at once, not a single steady push but a constant churning chaos that wanted me on my back, wanted me spinning downstream, wanted me gone. My dress billowed and dragged, a sail catching the wrong wind. The package under my dress pressed against my ribs. *Hold. Please hold.*

The water hit my chin.

My feet were going numb. I couldn't feel my fingers. I tried to focus on the fence ahead, on the gap, on the gap, keep your eyes on the gap, but the current kept nudging me sideways and I had to fight for every inch and my legs were shaking so hard I didn't know how much longer they'd hold.

Don't fall. If you fall it's over.

I reached the fence. Up close it was worse than I'd imagined; the gap narrower, the current down here at the base meaner and faster, compressed between the wire and the riverbed into something that felt almost solid, almost angry. The chain-link loomed over me, the posts disappearing down into black water. Somewhere behind me, through the trees, the compound existed. Father Michael existed. The white room existed.

I took one breath.

Held it.

And went under.

The silence was absolute. The cold was a different thing entirely down here, not cold but absence, the total removal of warmth from every cell of my body simultaneously. The current grabbed me the instant I submerged and wrenched me sideways with a force I hadn't expected, spinning me so I didn't know which way was up, my shoulder driving into the riverbed, rocks scraping along my arm. I couldn't see. I couldn't hear. I kicked toward where I thought the gap was and felt the fence graze my cheek instead, the metal edge sharp enough to sting even through the numbness.

Wrong way. Wrong way.

I twisted, pulled, got my hands on the chain-link and used it to orient myself. My lungs were already burning. I'd been under ten seconds, maybe fifteen. I found the gap with my hands and drove my body through it headfirst and the fence caught me.

The dress. Snagged on the wire somewhere at my hip, the fabric twisted and pinned, and I was stuck, half through and half not, the current on the far side pulling at my arms and the wire on the near side holding the rest of me and my lungs were past burning now, into a deeper register, a screaming that had no sound.

I pulled. The dress held.

I'm going to drown here. Right here, ten feet from freedom, I am going to drown and they'll find me tangled in their fence and Father Michael will say I chose this, will say my selfhood was the death of me, will use me as a lesson for every girl who comes after—

I stopped pulling against it and pushed sideways instead, an inch, two inches, feeling for slack in the fabric, and there, a fraction of give where the wire had snagged on a seam rather than the body of the dress itself.

I wrenched myself sideways and pulled with everything left in me.

The seam gave with a tear I felt in my teeth, and then I was through, tumbling and spinning in the current on the free side of the fence, and I didn't know up from down until my shoulder hit the riverbed again and I used it to push.

I broke the surface.

The sound came back like a slap; the river, the birds, the wind in the trees, the ragged terrible sound of my own breathing as I hauled air into lungs that had completely forgotten their function. The current dragged me downstream, fast, faster than I expected, and I couldn't find my feet, couldn't stand, just churned and gasped until my outstretched hand found a low-hanging branch and my fingers locked around it by pure reflex.

I pulled myself toward the bank one handhold at a time. My arms had nothing left. I used them anyway.

I collapsed face-down in the mud on the far bank and lay completely still.

My whole body shook. I couldn't stop it and I didn't try. I pressed my cheek into the cold wet earth and breathed in ragged pulls, each one a small victory, each one proof that I was still here, still alive, still on the right side of the fence.

Behind me through the trees I could just make out the white walls of the compound. The prayer hall roof. The neat garden beds where girls moved like ghosts in the morning light.

I pressed my face deeper into the mud and breathed.

I was out.

Slowly, with hands that barely worked, I pulled the plastic package from under my soaked dress. The wrapper had held. The book was dry.

The money intact. I pressed it against my chest like it was the most precious thing in the world, because right now it was, it was all there was, and I pushed myself to my feet with my arms shaking and my legs barely answering.

I ran into the trees.

I did not look back.

CHAPTER 8

Freya

I ran until my body stopped letting me.

Branches whipped at my face and arms, catching in my wet hair, tearing at my already-ruined dress. Somewhere in the first frantic minutes I'd lost the compound's thin canvas shoes, couldn't bear the way they squelched and slipped, and now the forest floor came up through the soles of my bare feet with every step; roots, stones, pine needles like nails, the cold wet earth. I stumbled twice, caught myself both times, kept moving. My lungs burned. My knees, still raw from the prayer hall floorboards, screamed. The book pressed against my ribs like a second heartbeat.

I couldn't slow down. Every snapped branch was an enforcer behind me. Every shift in the wind was a voice calling my name. I knew how they worked; Thomas with his cold patience,

James with his predator's stillness. And Andre, the one who never prayed and never smiled and watched from the edges with eyes that missed nothing. They'd find the gap in the fence. They'd see my footprints in the mud. They'd be fast and systematic and they had done this before.

I pushed harder, past the point where my body was making requests and into the territory where it was simply filing complaints I had no intention of honouring.

The trees grew thicker, the canopy closing overhead until the world became a dim green twilight. The river sounds faded. In their place; rustling leaves, birds I couldn't name, the creak of branches, the aliveness of a forest that had no interest in whether I survived it. I had never been alone in woods before. In the compound we only went outside in supervised groups, always within sight of the fence, the wilderness beyond existing only as a backdrop.

Now I was inside it and it was enormous and it didn't care about me at all.

The smell alone was overwhelming; damp earth and rotting leaves and pine sap and something musky underneath that my city-raised nose had no name for. Everything was too much, too close, too wild. I didn't know which direction I was moving. I only knew away, and away was the only direction that mattered.

My foot caught a root.

I went down hard, palms slamming into

the dirt, knees hitting stone. Pain shot up my legs, immediate and white-hot, and I pressed my mouth shut and stayed there on my hands and knees, breathing, tasting copper where I'd bitten my tongue.

I looked at my hands. Scraped raw, embedded with grit and debris, already swelling. My knees throbbed through the torn fabric; I could feel the warm wet of blood soaking through. I pressed my palms to my face and the dirt smeared across my cheeks and mixed with tears I hadn't realised I was shedding.

Stop. Just for a moment. Stop.

I sat back and let myself shake.

My muscles had been screaming for the last ten minutes of running. My bare feet throbbed with a pain that had been overridden by terror until this exact moment, arriving back all at once with every penny of interest accumulated.

I'd left.

I had actually left.

The compound had been my entire world for weeks; the cabins and the prayer hall and the garden beds, the schedule and the chanting and the smell of beeswax. The certainty of it. The terrible comfort of knowing exactly what came next. And now it was gone and I was alone in a forest in a ruined dress with sixty-three dollars and a children's book, and the question arrived before I could stop it;

What have I done?

Sarah's eyes answered before anything else could. That soft unfocused blankness, the smile that had nothing behind it, the way she moved through the compound like a person who had been carefully emptied and filled with something else. That would have been me. Another few weeks of white rooms and chanting and the phrase drilling into my bones in the dark, and that would have been exactly me.

The question dissolved.

I made myself think. I couldn't run blindly forever; I needed direction, a plan, something better than away. The compound had to be accessible from somewhere; they brought in supplies, had visitors, existed in the world even while pretending to be apart from it. There had to be a town nearby. People. I just had to find them.

I looked around, trying to orient myself. The trees all looked the same; tall pines, rough bark, the ground thick with fallen needles and moss. No path. No trail. No sound of traffic.

I held my breath and listened. Wind through branches. A crow somewhere to the north. The rustle of something small in the underbrush. No voices. No footsteps.

Not yet.

The light was brighter in one direction; not by much, but enough. The trees might be thinning. Or it might be wishful thinking. I had no way to know which.

I unwrapped the package one more time, checking with hands that were still shaking. The book dry, the money intact. Sixty-three dollars between me and everything. I wrapped it back carefully and pressed it against my stomach.

I thought of Lucy stepping into the wardrobe. Not knowing what was on the other side. Going anyway, because staying in the known world was its own kind of surrender.

I stood up. My knees nearly sent me back down. I locked them and breathed through it and stayed upright.

Then I turned toward the light and started walking.

CHAPTER 9

Freya

My clothes dried as I walked but the cold stayed in my bones.

The highway shoulder was uneven and cruel under bare feet, loose gravel and cracked asphalt that bit into my soles with every step. I kept to the grass where I could, wet and cold and marginally kinder, and I walked with my eyes on the horizon and my arms wrapped around the plastic package pressed against my stomach and I did not think about what was behind me. Only what was ahead.

The lights of the town appeared gradually; orange smears against the grey sky that sharpened, as I got closer, into neon signs and streetlamps and the glow of a world that didn't know I existed. I stopped at the edge of it, at the place where the highway shoulder became a proper pavement, and I stood there and breathed.

People. Moving, talking, existing. A woman walked a dog. A teenager on a skateboard clattered over a pavement crack. A car alarm shrieked somewhere down the block and I flinched so hard my shoulder blades slammed together.

In the compound, the only sounds were bells and prayers and the whisper of fabric on floorboards. Here the world just screamed, indifferent and continuous, and no one flinched at any of it.

I pressed myself against the brick of the nearest building and let the rough texture scrape through the thin fabric of my dress. My heart pounded behind my ribs. I counted things to slow it; the cracks in the pavement, the parked cars, the pigeons on the shopfront opposite. Just a town. Just people. No one was watching me.

I needed clothes.

The dress I was wearing was a ruin; blue cotton stained with river mud and blood, the fabric torn at the hip where the fence had caught it. I looked like what I was. I couldn't afford to look like what I was.

I found a thrift store on a corner, its window painted with cheerful letters; *Treasures.* The bell above the door dinged when I pushed through and the smell hit me first; dust and old fabric and detergent, nothing like the beeswax and chemical sweetness of the prayer hall. I stood just inside the door with my back to the glass and stared.

Racks. Rows and rows of racks stretching back into the store, jackets hanging from long arms, sweaters piled in bins, shelves of shoes and belts and tables cluttered with mugs and trinkets. A radio somewhere played tinny music I didn't recognise. The fluorescent lights overhead buzzed at a frequency that felt like it was drilling into the back of my eyes.

In the compound we had a wardrobe. Four dresses. One pair of shoes. A hairbrush. That was it. Here there was enough clothing in a single room to dress every woman in the compound five times over, and the sheer volume of it made my head swim.

I moved deeper into the maze before I could freeze entirely. My fingers found a rack of t-shirts, faded soft cotton, and then a blue hoodie, thick and warm and real. I held it against my chest. It would cover me. It would make me invisible.

A man with a name tag that read *Jim* appeared at my elbow with a pricing gun in his hand and I spun around before I could stop myself, my heart slamming against my ribs. He was just a man. A civilian. But for one terrible second the shape of the object in his hand sent a spike of pure terror through me that I felt in my back teeth.

"Need a dressing room?" he asked.

"No," I managed. "I'm okay."

He shrugged and walked away. I turned back

to the rack, my hands shaking, and made myself choose. Dark jeans, heavy and stiff. Thick wool socks. The grey long-sleeved shirt. The blue hoodie. I clutched them to my chest in a pile so large I could barely see over it and shuffled toward the counter.

The girl with pink hair scanned everything with quick beeps.

"Twenty-three fifty," she said.

I fumbled with the bills I'd moved to my pocket. My hands were sweating, the paper damp, the numbers blurring. In the compound, we didn't pay for things. We just existed. Father Michael taught us that currency was corruption, that the exchange of money poisoned the soul. Standing here with crumpled bills in my shaking hands, I felt the full weight of that ignorance; I didn't know what things cost. I didn't know if I had enough. I could see it unfolding already, her hand reaching for a phone, security appearing, questions I couldn't answer.

I shoved the pile of bills across the counter.

She counted with fast fingers. Then she looked at me. Her eyes moved over my bruised face, the scrapes and cuts visible under the ruins of the dress, the dirt still caught in the hollows of my throat.

"Close enough," she said, and swept the money into the drawer. She stuffed the clothes into a plastic bag and held it out. "Next."

I took the bag and walked out into the afternoon sun.

* * * *

I needed somewhere to change. I turned away from the main street, looking for an alley, a quiet corner, anything, and turned a corner and stopped dead.

A police cruiser sat at the curb. Lights off, engine idling. Inside, an officer drank coffee and talked on his radio, not looking at anything in particular, not looking for me.

I couldn't move.

My feet went to concrete. My vision tunnelled, the edges of the world going dark and hazy, the sound of the radio crackling through the cruiser window becoming the only sound in the universe. He shifted in his seat and I bit down on my tongue so hard I tasted copper.

He was just a man. Just a police officer drinking coffee. My body didn't care. My body had learned one thing in the compound with a thoroughness that went all the way down to the bone; men with authority were not safe. The enforcers wore black and carried rifles and walked the fence lines. This officer was a different kind of authority entirely, and the difference didn't register anywhere that mattered. He was between me and the edge of town and my mind was already constructing it; he'd see me, he'd stop me, he'd ask questions, he'd call someone, and wherever I ended up it would not be free.

I ducked behind a mailbox, pressing myself

against the cold metal, dragging the plastic bag tight against my legs. I squeezed my eyes shut and waited for boots on pavement.

Nothing.

I peeked around the edge. He was eating a donut. Still on his radio. Still not looking at me.

I turned and went the other way, cutting through an alleyway behind a laundromat, and ran until the cruiser was far enough behind me that I could breathe again. I found a small public restroom near a park; a cinderblock building with chipped paint and a lock that actually worked. I shut myself in the stall.

My hands shook so badly I had to rip the plastic bag open with my teeth. I took off the dress and let it fall to the dirty floor. My body underneath was a map of what the last few hours had done; the friction burn from the fence wrapping around my ribs, the scrapes on my knees dark and raw, my feet cut and dirty from the forest floor.

I pulled on the wool socks first. They hurt where they pressed against the open skin of my feet, and then they were warm, and warmth was so foreign after everything that I stood still for a moment just feeling it.

Jeans. Grey shirt. The blue hoodie over everything.

I stood in front of the dirty mirror over the sink while the fluorescent bulb flickered overhead. My hair hung in tangles around my face.

There were shadows under my eyes. My lips were chapped and pale.

But the girl in the mirror wasn't wearing a pastel dress. She wasn't wearing a silver compass. She had messy hair and terrified eyes and she looked, against all odds, like she belonged in this loud, chaotic world.

I picked up the ruined dress from the floor. I should leave it. It was evidence. But I folded it small and tight and shoved it to the bottom of the plastic bag anyway. Then I picked up the book and rubbed my thumb over the lion on the cover.

"Okay," I whispered to the girl in the mirror. "Just walk."

I pulled the hood up, shoved my hands into the pockets, and stepped back out into the street.

CHAPTER 10

Freya

The vacancy sign was buzzing orange when I finally found the motel.

I had walked for maybe twenty minutes after leaving the park restroom, following the highway east with my hood up and my eyes down, and by the time the neon light smeared itself across my vision I was walking on will alone. My feet had stopped sending clear signals. Now they just sent one; stop.

The clerk at the front desk had greasy hair and eyes fixed on a small television mounted in the corner. He didn't look at me when I pushed through the door. He didn't look at me when I put the crumpled bills on the counter. He slid a key across without a word and went back to his programme.

Room 104.

I locked the deadbolt. Threw the chain. Stood

in the centre of the room and breathed.

The bed had a synthetic comforter that smelled of starch and old cigarettes and it was the most beautiful thing I had ever seen in my life. I sat on the edge of it and the mattress sank under my weight and I sat there for a long moment just letting that happen; the give of it, the softness, the fact that no one was going to tell me to get up.

Then I dragged myself into the bathroom.

* * * *

The shower stall was narrow, the tile yellowed with age. I turned the handle and waited. When the water came it wasn't timed. It wasn't lukewarm. It steamed and hissed, hot and immediate, and I stepped in and didn't wash. I just stood under the spray with my eyes closed and my hands hanging at my sides.

No one was timing me. No one was standing at the door counting the minutes. I could stand here until the water ran cold and no one would say a word about it.

The water ran red with blood.

I watched it spiral down the drain, pink and then paler and then finally clear, and that was when the tears came. They mixed with the shower water and I couldn't have said where one ended and the other began, and I didn't try. I just stood there and let everything I hadn't been able to feel for the last few hours come through at once; the river, the fence, the cold, the forest floor under my bare feet, the pink-haired girl saying *close enough* like it was nothing, like small mercies happened every day.

I scrubbed until my skin was pink and raw. I turned off the water and the silence of the motel rushed back in.

I stepped out onto the bathmat and gripped the sink until my legs stopped shaking.

The mirror showed me the full inventory. Bruises everywhere; my shoulder was a deep mottled purple where it had driven into the riverbed twice, dark smudges mapped across my knees and hips where I'd hit stone and earth in the forest. My knees were a mess of scraped raw skin on top of the bruising. My palms were cut and swollen, stinging when I flexed my fingers. I lifted my arm and turned; the friction burn from the fence wrapped around my ribs and hip, an angry abraded stripe that was already darkening at the edges.

I found the first aid kit in the medicine cabinet behind a hairdryer with a frayed cord and a row of complimentary shampoos. Small white box with a red cross. I sat down on the closed toilet lid and opened it.

Alcohol wipes. Butterfly bandages. A small tube of antibiotic ointment. A roll of gauze.

I started with my hands. The shower had done the cleaning; now it was about infection. I ran the alcohol wipe carefully over each palm, working it into the cuts, and pressed the butterfly bandages over the deepest splits to hold the skin together.

My knees next. I applied the ointment carefully, with a gentleness I hadn't used on myself in a long time. In the compound, pain from a correction was expected to linger; treating it would have been a small rebellion. I placed butterfly bandages over the deepest gouges and pressed until the bleeding slowed.

Finally, my feet.

I lifted one foot and rested my heel on the edge of the tub. The soles were raw and red, patches of skin missing where the forest floor had taken them. I cleaned them slowly, hissing through my teeth at the alcohol burn, and wrapped gauze around each arch and secured it with tape.

I stood up carefully and tested my weight. My feet held.

I looked down at the bandages; white and clumsy against my bruised skin. Ugly. Mine. No one had told me how to do this. No one had told me to smile through it.

I walked back into the main room, turned off the overhead light, and got into bed.

The neon sign outside bled through the thin curtains in rhythmic pulses of red and orange. I lay on my back and watched the light move across the ceiling and told myself I was safe. The deadbolt was thrown. The chain was latched. No one knew I was here.

I was asleep before I finished the thought.

* * * *

The darkness behind my eyelids wasn't empty.

I was in the white room.

Not the garden. Not the cabins. The room at the top of the hill, the one I'd only ever seen in fragments; the door with the heavy lock, the light that was wrong. The walls were white. The floor was white. The ceiling was white. No windows. Just strips of fluorescent light embedded in the plaster, humming at a frequency that made my teeth ache.

I was kneeling. My legs were folded beneath me, my hands resting on my thighs. I couldn't feel my own muscles. My limbs were heavy and distant, belonging to someone else.

Father Michael sat in a wooden chair in the centre of the room. He wasn't wearing his robes. He was in a black suit, sharp and wrong, and when he looked at me his face was patient and unhurried and completely certain.

"You have so much noise in you, Freya," he said. His voice didn't echo. It came from inside my skull. "The world puts noise in there. Fear. Confusion. Survival." He stood without seeming to move and was suddenly in front of me. "We are going to take it out."

I tried to shake my head. My throat was closed. My jaw was wired shut.

"The water didn't wash it away," he said, his

hand hovering over my forehead. His palm was smooth and pale. "The running didn't wash it away."

He lowered his hand.

The moment his skin touched mine the white static exploded. It wasn't pain. It was a flood, filling every crack and crevice until the pressure was unbearable. I felt the panic from the river evaporate. The defiance from the fence snap. The memory of my mother's voice dulled, muffled, gone. I was being erased. *Let me go,* I thought, but the thought didn't finish. It just dissolved into the hum.

"You will become one with us all."

He was chanting it now. Each repetition drove deeper. I felt my awareness compressing, shrinking to a point of light in a vast white ocean. The part of me that loved books. The part of me that wanted to live. The part of me that was Freya. Being scooped out. Leaving a hollow clean space behind.

"No," I tried to say. It came out as a whimper.

"Yes," he corrected. His other hand moved to my throat. He didn't squeeze. He just rested his fingers there, possessing the airway, the breath, the life.

"Empty," he whispered. "And be filled."

The white light went blinding. It consumed the room, consumed him, consumed me. I was dissolving. I was becoming the hum. I was becoming—

Freya.

A voice from outside the white, screaming my name. It sounded like me but stronger. Louder. A version of me that hadn't let go yet.

Wake up.

I hit the floor.

I had rolled clean out of the bed, tangled in the sheets, and crashed onto the thin carpet, and I lay there gasping with my heart slamming so hard behind my ribs I thought I might be sick. My skin was slick with cold sweat. I grabbed the fabric of my t-shirt and yanked it away from my throat, needing air, needing to feel that my throat was mine.

I slapped my own cheeks. Hard.

The sting was immediate. Sharp. Real.

"Ow," I choked.

Real.

I scrambled backward until my spine hit the edge of the bed and pulled my knees up to my chest and looked around the room. The neon light pulsed. The dresser. The TV. The door with the deadbolt and the chain. I was in Room 104. I was in the motel. I was out.

The bandages on my hands were still there.

I pressed my face into my knees and breathed in the smell of stale detergent and my own sweat and I swore, quietly and completely, that I would burn everything down before I let them put me back in that chair.

* * * *

I couldn't sleep after that.

I sat on the edge of the bed with the lamp already on and the book in my lap and I thought about Andre.

I didn't want to. He arrived in my head the way bad things always arrived after dark; uninvited, taking up more space than they had any right to. I remembered him from the compound the way you remember something that frightened you before you understood why. He stood at the edges of gatherings, never quite among the worshippers. He didn't pray. He didn't smile. He just watched, his eyes moving over the hall and the paths and the perimeter with a steadiness that was different from the other enforcers; they watched the girls. He watched the compound itself.

The girls whispered about him. Brought there as a child, they said. Raised inside the fence. The leader's hand.

I remembered the weight of his gaze across a room. The way it landed on you and didn't move on.

I looked at the door. At the deadbolt. At the chain.

I told myself; miles away. I crossed the river. I paid cash. I left no trail.

I watched the door handle and waited for dawn.

CHAPTER 11

Andre

I found her trail at the riverbank.

The mud on the far side held everything; the drag marks where she'd hauled herself out, the uneven impressions of bare feet, the deep gouge where her knee had hit when she collapsed. I crouched and pressed two fingers into the nearest print. The edges were still sharp. The water hadn't softened them yet.

Two hours. Maybe three.

She was hurt. The footprints told me that much without trying; her left side was favoring, the impressions uneven, the right foot landing harder and more deliberately than the left. She was compensating. Moving through pain she didn't have the luxury of stopping for.

I straightened and followed the trail into the trees.

Father Michael had given the order before I'd

even made it back from the prayer hall the night she ran. Bring her back. Reintegration. The vocabulary of cruelty always couched in something cleaner. I had taken the mission the way I took every mission; without comment, without feeling, the way you do when feeling has stopped being something you can afford.

I had brought back three runners in the past two years. The process was mechanical. Read the trail, find the girl, return the problem to the man who owned it. I didn't think about what happened after. My mother's safety lived on the other side of my usefulness, and that was the only calculation that had ever mattered.

I told myself this was the same.

The trail was sloppy and frantic, a story written in broken ferns and scuffed earth. Here she'd stumbled, catching herself on a tree trunk; I could see the smear of mud from her palm. There she'd fallen hard, the impression of both knees still visible in the soft dirt, deeper on the right than the left. I ran my fingers over the disturbed ground. Fresh pine needles scattered where they shouldn't be. She'd been moving fast, too fast for someone with no shoes and no idea where she was going.

Away, the trail said. *Just away.*

I knew that feeling. I'd never acted on it, but I knew it.

She'd shed the canvas shoes somewhere in the first mile; I found them in a patch of undergrowth, waterlogged and useless, discarded without ceremony. Bare feet from here on. Through roots and stones and the cold wet forest floor. I looked at the ground ahead and felt something tighten in my chest that I immediately classified as professional concern. A girl with damaged feet moved slowly. Slowly meant visible. Visible meant someone else found her first, and the kind of someone who found a young woman alone and barefoot on a highway shoulder at dawn was not always the lesser problem.

I moved faster.

The trees thinned as the highway approached. I heard the traffic before I saw the asphalt, that low continuous hum of the outside world that I'd spent years keeping the girls away from. I stopped at the tree line and scanned the road in both directions.

There. A figure on the shoulder, moving east. Blue dress, dark hair. Walking with her arms wrapped around something pressed against her stomach.

She didn't know I was behind her. She was watching the horizon with the focused desperation of someone who had decided that looking back would stop her feet entirely.

I stayed in the tree line and matched her pace.

* * * *

The town was small; a single main street,

a few dozen buildings, the particular quietness of a place that folded in on itself after dark. I watched her from a distance as she moved through it. She flinched at a car alarm. She pressed herself against a brick wall and stood there breathing with her eyes closed and her hands flat against the surface. I was close enough to see her lips moving.

She was managing. Barely. But managing.

I watched her go into the thrift store and I stayed across the street with my hands in my pockets and noted the time. I watched her come out with a plastic bag and a slightly steadier walk. I watched the police cruiser at the corner send her bolting down an alleyway at a pace her feet could not have enjoyed.

I could have taken her any of those moments. That was the job; find and retrieve, minimum disruption. But Father Michael had been clear; he wanted her to understand there was nowhere his reach didn't extend. That there was no world outside the compass points. That was a different kind of work, and it required patience.

I found the motel before she did. A single-story building off the highway, a vacancy sign buzzing orange in the grey afternoon light. I bought coffee from the machine in the lobby with coins from my pocket and stood in the shadow of the ice machine and watched the parking lot until she appeared at the far end of it, limping, the hood of a blue sweatshirt pulled up, her arms still wrapped around whatever she was protecting.

She went to the office. Came out with a key. Room 104.

I finished my coffee and waited for the light under her door to go out.

* * * *

She left at eleven. The Do Not Disturb sign swung on the handle as she pulled the door shut behind her. I watched her from the corner of the building, her shoulders hunched against the night air, moving in the direction of the fast food place two blocks down. She walked like every step cost something she wasn't sure she had.

My window was approximately half an hour.

I crossed the parking lot without hurrying. The door to Room 104 was cheap hollow-core wood, the paint faded, the number screwed on slightly crooked. I stood in front of it for a moment and took out my knife.

Father Michael wanted her to understand there was nowhere his reach didn't extend. The how of that was mine to decide. I looked at the door and thought about what would land deepest, what would cut through the relief of clean clothes and a locked room and a full stomach and remind her of exactly what she'd come from.

The symbol.

I pressed the tip of the blade against the wood.

The first stroke was the circle. The blade bit

deep, peeling back thin curls of painted wood, the sound of it a slow scrape in the quiet night. Then the four points. North. South. East. West. Each one deliberate, each one dragging through the soft wood with a patience that Father Michael would have called devotion.

I carved it deep. Deep enough that she wouldn't mistake it for random damage, wouldn't talk herself into believing it was already there. Deep enough that the number 104 split down the middle, bisected cleanly. A signature. A promise.

There is no direction where we are not with you.

I put the knife away and stepped back.

The symbol stared back at me from the door, pale raw wood showing through the stain, and I felt nothing that resembled satisfaction. What I felt instead was a low uncomfortable awareness, like a splinter working itself deeper, that the girl inside that room had crossed a river alone and barefoot and with nothing but a children's book, and I was standing outside her door in the dark carving cult symbols into the wood to make sure she knew she hadn't gotten far enough.

I walked back around the corner and found a shadow and settled in to wait.

She came back half an hour later, a grease-spotted bag in her hand, her shoulders looser than when she'd left. She was walking almost normally despite the feet.

Then she looked up and saw the door.

I watched her freeze. Watched the bag slip from her fingers and hit the concrete without her registering it. Watched her hand go to her throat, reaching for the necklace that wasn't there anymore, finding nothing. Watched her stand completely motionless on the cheap welcome mat while her body processed what her mind already knew.

She'd been found.

I watched her go inside. I listened to the sounds through the thin door; the deadbolt, the chain, the muffled sounds of someone moving too fast and breathing too hard. She was packing. She thought she had seconds to run.

I waited until the movement inside slowed.

Then I drove my heel into the door just above the handle.

CHAPTER 12

Freya

Hunger was a sharper pain than the bruises, a gnawing hollow in my stomach that eventually outweighed the terror.

When I could no longer stand the shaking in my hands, I left the motel room. I hung the Do Not Disturb sign on the knob, a flimsy plastic shield against the world, and headed for the fast food place two blocks down. It was late, probably around eleven, and the world around me was dead quiet. It was slow going. Every step was a jarring reminder of the river and the fence; my feet throbbed with a dull relentless agony, and the bandages around my palms made clutching the few dollars I had difficult. The sidewalk was cracked and unforgiving. Halfway there I had to stop. I leaned against the rough brick of a closed laundromat, squeezed my eyes shut against a wave of nausea, and waited for the stitch in my side to ease.

"You okay, honey?"

I looked up. A middle-aged woman with a shopping bag, her brow furrowed. Her eyes swept over my dishevelled hair, the bruise on my arm, the way I was favouring my left side. Panic seized my throat. If I engage, if I let her help, she might ask questions. She might call the police. The police might take me back.

"I'm fine," I said, my voice too tight, forcing a smile that felt more like a grimace. "Just twisted my ankle. I'm fine."

She hesitated. She could see the wildness in my eyes, I knew she could. She took a step back and raised her hands slightly.

"Alright then. Take care of yourself." She walked away quickly.

I watched her disappear around the corner and waited for my heart to slow. My lungs felt too small. The encounter left me rattled in a way I hadn't expected; kindness felt dangerous. In the compound, kindness always had strings attached. It was transactional, conditional, a tool. Father Michael's gentle voice before the correction. The soft touch before the isolation. I didn't know how to accept concern without waiting for the other shoe to drop.

I pushed off the wall and kept moving.

****

The Burger King was twenty-four hours. The

air inside was thick with salt and grease and I stepped up to the counter with my hands trembling so hard I nearly dropped the crumpled bills.

"Welcome in, what can I get you?" the cashier asked.

I stared at the board. Burgers. Chicken nuggets. Fish sandwiches. Salads. Fries. Large, medium, small. With cheese. Without cheese. Too many choices. My mind blanked. The fluorescent lights hummed overhead, making the pictures on the menu swim. Each image was aggressively cheerful; burgers with perfect sesame seeds, fries golden and crisp, milkshakes thick and creamy. My stomach twisted with hunger and confusion. What if I chose wrong? What if I picked something I couldn't eat and wasted what little money I had left? In the compound, we had no choices. We ate what was served. Here, I had to decide the composition of my own meal, and the pressure of it was paralysing.

The cashier's fingers began tapping impatiently against his screen.

"Just a burger?" he prompted, raising an eyebrow. "Ma'am?"

"I want the number four," I blurted, pointing at the picture of the chicken sandwich. "And a Coke. Large."

"Anything else?"

I shook my head, terrified to ask for more. But as I stepped aside to wait, I looked back at the menu. I could have picked anything. I must have looked insane, standing there staring at a fast food menu with tears in my eyes. But I didn't care. The sheer volume of available calories, the freedom to choose grease over gruel, it felt like a miracle. I could walk back up there and order ten burgers if I had the money and no one would stop me.

I grabbed the grease-spotted bag and walked out.

I kept my head down and counted my steps. One, two, three. The sidewalk cracked under my feet, the air thick with frying oil and exhaust. A group of teenagers passed me, laughing too loud, their voices sharp and jarring. I pressed myself against a storefront and waited for them to move on. My hand tightened around the paper bag, the grease seeping through to my palm. Every shadow felt like a threat. Every set of headlights sweeping the pavement made me freeze. In the compound, I had known where the danger was. It wore white robes and carried silver compasses. Out here, danger could be anyone, anywhere. Every time a car slowed, my heart seized against my ribs.

I felt like a ghost wearing a stolen skin.

By the time I reached the motel, the bag was cooling in my palm and my skin was humming with dread. The moon cast long shadows across the parking lot, turning the neon vacancy sign into a flickering bruise. I was nearly at my door before I saw it.

I stopped dead.

My keys rattled in my hand, the sound too loud in the quiet night. My eyes locked onto the wood and the world tilted. It wasn't a mark. It wasn't damage or something left by a previous guest.

It was a compass.

A circle with four points, jagged and violent, the wood frayed around each gouge like torn flesh. It cut clean through the painted 104 like a brand, a reminder, a promise.

Loyalty. Perfection. Worship. Truth.

The paper bag slipped from my fingers. It hit the concrete with a muted thud. My hand reached out, trembling, fingers hovering an inch from the gouges. I could feel the violence in the cuts, the deliberate brutality of each stroke. Someone had stood here. Someone had carved this into my door while I was gone. Someone knew exactly where I was.

How? When? I was careful. I paid cash. I didn't speak to anyone. My mind raced, a chaotic carousel of horrors. The paranoia I had felt on the walk back wasn't just anxiety; it was instinct. I was never alone. The eyes were always there. North, South, East, West. The compass points spun in my vision and Father Michael's voice arrived fully formed; there is no direction where we are not with you. The compound gates. Morning assemblies. The silver necklaces every member wore. Those curves and lines were burned into my brain, etched into my consciousness for weeks, and now they were on my door.

The symbol told me I had been found.

The chokehold tightened. Not a hand; the ideology itself, wrapping around my throat, squeezing until I felt small again. I was just a girl in a pastel dress. I was property. I was a defect that needed correction. The freedom I had tasted was just a dream I was waking up from.

The freeze shattered.

I couldn't run into the parking lot, too exposed on the open asphalt. I bolted into the room and slammed the door. The lock. The deadbolt. The chain, my hands jerky and frantic, my breath coming in high thin gasps. But the wood felt paper-thin now, and I knew exactly what kind of blade had made those gouges.

The room that had felt like a sanctuary felt like a trap.

I grabbed the plastic bag from the bathroom and started shoving everything inside. Every bruise on my body throbbed in time with my pulse. I couldn't leave the book. It lay on the bed, the last thread connecting me to the person I had been before Father Michael's voice started rewriting my mind. I snatched it up and shoved it into the bag.

A crash sounded behind me.

"You're loud."

The voice was a low rumble, like a car engine idling just feet away. I spun around, a cry dying in my throat. The door hung by its hinges. He stood between me and the exit, filling the narrow room with his body alone. Dark clothes, no compound whites. A hard jaw shadowed with stubble. Eyes that didn't just look; they catalogued everything in a single breath.

I recognised him before my mind had words for it. The ghost at the compound's spine. The rumour wrapped in flesh. He was not the leader. He was not one of the hollow-eyed faithful. But he was the cult's blade, and his presence meant the leader's will had followed me out here into the world.

He didn't move to grab me. He just watched, his posture easy, a predator in no hurry to strike. His gaze dropped to the book in my hands and his mouth curved into something that was not quite a smile.

"Got yourself caught because of a story, didn't you?" Low. Unnervingly calm. "You really thought you could run, little bird?"

The mockery cut through my pride and left me raw. He could see all of it; the desperation, the attachment to a childish fantasy, the foolish hope. He could snatch the book from my hands right now. But he didn't. He just noted it, filed it away, and said the words that closed around me like a fist.

"It's time to come back now, little bird."

CHAPTER 13

Andre

I had every advantage.

The layout of the room was a dead end. She was alone, unarmed, and shaking so hard I could hear her teeth chattering from the doorway. The cult symbol I'd carved into the cheap wood, a jagged compass pointing to nowhere, had been a warning and a claim. I'd marked her as mine to retrieve.

I should have been able to haul her out by the wrist and march her straight back to the forest, to the leader, to the river she'd crawled through. It should have been a ten-minute operation. Grab. Drag. Done.

I'd done this before. Runaways always came back, some willingly, some in pieces. The process was mechanical. Clinical. I didn't think about the girls as people; they were problems to solve, tasks to complete. Father Michael gave the orders. I executed them. My mother had been drowning when the compound found us both; broken and lost in a world that had no use for us. Father Michael had given her purpose, safety, a place to belong. The least I could do was serve.

This should have been the same.

Instead, the mission began to fracture the moment our eyes met.

She didn't cower. She didn't drop to her knees and beg for forgiveness like the others. She looked at me and I saw the calculation behind the fear. She was measuring the distance to the window, the weight of the book in her hand, the angle of my stance.

Smart. Too smart for her own good.

"You don't have to do this," she said, her voice trembling but clear.

"It's already done, Freya," I said, stepping into the room. "Come quietly. Save yourself the pain."

She hurled the book.

It wasn't a desperate toss; it was a fastball aimed right at my head. I ducked, the paperback thudding against the doorframe behind me. Before I could straighten, she lunged.

She tried to fight her way past, kicking at my shins, clawing at my eyes, snapping her teeth like a cornered animal. I caught her wrists, spinning her around, but she twisted like an eel and drove an elbow hard into my ribs.

I grunted. More in surprise than pain.

I was impressed.

God help me, I was impressed.

The girls at the compound were soft clay by now, baked in the oven of obedience until they were hard and brittle. But Freya? She was raw, jagged stone. She fought like she had nothing to lose. Like going back was worse than dying in this room. And maybe it was. I'd seen what Father Michael did to the ones who ran. I'd stood guard during the reintegration sessions, listening to prayers that sounded more like breaking than healing.

I shoved the thought aside. Not my problem. My job was retrieval, not judgment.

"Is that all you have?" I taunted, keeping my voice low, holding her off with one arm while she rained blows against my chest. "The leader said you were trouble. He didn't say you were scrappy."

"Get. Off. Me."

She slammed her heel down on my instep. That one actually hurt. I used the flash of pain as a pivot, crowding her backward, walking her until her spine hit the wall and I had my weight against her.

Chest to chest. Her breath came in short sharp gasps against my neck.

The air left the room.

Or maybe it was just mine.

I expected the terror to take over. I expected her to go still the way they always went still when the fight drained out. But she didn't. She looked up at me and the calculation was still running behind her eyes, the fury still burning, still looking for the next opening.

Her face was flushed, a streak of dirt marking her cheekbone, her eyes blazing with a fury that made my blood run hot. Her lips were parted, her chest heaving against mine with each ragged breath. This close I could see the pulse jumping in her throat, wild and frantic.

It was wrong.

It was a betrayal of everything I was raised to be.

But as I held her there, pinning her wrists to the wall, I felt something shift in my chest. Not attraction, I refused to call it that. It was more like recognition. Like looking at someone and seeing the outline of something I'd buried so deep I'd forgotten it existed.

She was alive in a way I had forgotten how to be.

The heat of her body soaked through my shirt. The scent of pine and river water and wild terrified sweat filled my lungs. I was aware of every point where we touched; her wrists under my hands, her chest against mine, the way her hip pressed into my thigh.

My gaze dropped to her mouth. Just for a second. Just long enough to notice the way her bottom lip was slightly fuller than the top, the way it trembled with each exhale.

What the hell was wrong with me?

This was a retrieval. A job. She was cargo, not a person.

"You're strong," I murmured, the words slipping out before I could stop them. "For a little bird."

"I hate you," she spat, her voice cracking.

"I know." I couldn't stop the corner of my mouth from lifting. "You hate that I caught you. You hate that I'm stronger. And you hate that you're still looking at me like I'm the only real thing in this room."

She bared her teeth and lunged forward, trying to bite my jaw.

I caught her chin, forced her head back, my fingers against the line of her jaw. The contact was electric, a jolt that seared straight down my spine.

She stilled. Her chest heaved against mine, her pulse hammering wildly under my thumb.

For one insane second, I wanted to close the distance between us. Wanted to see if that defiant mouth tasted as fierce as it looked. Wanted to know if she'd bite me or kiss me back.

I shut the thought down hard.

"You're making a mistake," she whispered, her eyes locked on mine, searching for a crack. "I won't go back there. I'll die first."

"You won't die," I said, my voice rougher than I intended. "I won't let you."

She froze.

The admission hung between us, heavy and irretrievable. I watched the confusion move through her face, the slight hitch of her breath. I'd said too much. Let something through the armor that had no business getting through.

I cursed under my breath and spun her around, pulling her arms behind her back.

The moment shattered. The fight came roaring back, her elbows flying, feet scrabbling against the carpet. I pressed her against the dresser with my weight and wrestled her wrists together, and she kicked backward and connected with my knee, and I yanked the zip tie from my pocket and got it around her wrists and pulled it tight.

Then I stopped.

Her wrists were already bruised from the fence wire, dark against pale skin, and the zip tie was biting into it, leaving fresh red marks. Turning them behind her back would wrench her shoulders before we even reached the car. I'd done it before, to others. The protocol was clear; maximum restraint, minimum comfort. Pain taught obedience. Father Michael had said it enough times that I could recite it in my sleep.

I looked at the marks the tie was already leaving.

I cut it.

Before she could react I spun her around, pulled her arms in front of her, and re-tied them at her stomach.

She stared at me, breathing hard.

"Why?"

Good question. I didn't have an answer that wouldn't make me sound like something I couldn't afford to be.

"Get on the bed," I said. "Sit down. Don't move."

"I'm not your dog," she shot back, but the conviction had gone out of it. She was swaying slightly, the adrenaline draining out of her.

"No," I said, stepping back, putting the width of the room between us. "You're my responsibility. And right now my responsibility is finding a car without you throwing yourself into traffic."

I gestured to the faded mattress.

She sat. Slowly. Watching me every second.

I turned to the door. The frame was splintered, the deadbolt hanging loose. I put my hand on the knob.

"Try to run," I said, "and next time I tie you behind your back."

A beat of silence.

"I'm still running, Andre."

Her voice was quiet. Steady. I turned enough to see her; sitting on the edge of the mattress, wrists bound in front of her, testing the tie with small careful movements. Her eyes met mine and the fear was gone for a second, replaced by something that had no right to be as hard to look at as it was.

"You can chase me all you want," she said.

"I'm not yours to keep."

I stepped out into the night and pulled the ruined door shut behind me.

CHAPTER 14

Freya

The second the door clicked shut, I started counting. I had about sixty seconds before he might come back.

One.

I held my breath, my lungs burning, listening for the sound of his boots on the asphalt. For the heavy tread that would tell me he hadn't actually left, that he was just waiting on the other side of the thin wood, toying with me.

Two.

Nothing. Just the hum of the ice machine down the walkway, a mechanical rhythmic drone that had always been background noise and now sounded like a countdown.

A car door slammed in the distance, sharp and violent, and I flinched, squeezing my eyes shut. I waited for footsteps to turn toward my room.

They didn't. The car revved and drove away.

Three. Four.

My mind was racing, cataloguing options. The window? I'd checked it earlier. It opened, but barely, and the drop to the ground was at least ten feet. The door? I'd heard the deadbolt slide home when he pulled it shut.

The zip tie. That was the only option.

I scrambled off the bed, the plastic biting into my wrists. The kitchenette was tiny, a cramped space of cracked laminate and yellowing linoleum. I yanked the bottom drawer open with my bound hands, my movements jerky and desperate.

Cutlery. A paper napkin. And there, stuck in the back of the silverware tray, a pair of small dull scissors with orange handles.

My heart hammered against my ribs so hard I felt sick.

Thank God. Thank God for lazy motel cleaners who don't check drawers thoroughly.

I fumbled them open, my fingers slippery with sweat. The orange plastic handles were cheap, the kind that bent under pressure. But they had blades. Dull, but sharp enough.

I wedged the blade between my wrists and sawed.

Twelve. Thirteen.

The plastic was thick. The scissors were dull, biting into it more than slicing. Every creak in the floorboards, every whistle of wind through the window frame made me freeze, terrified it was him coming back.

What if this was a test? What if he was standing just outside, waiting to see what I'd do?

The scissors slipped, gouging the skin of my wrist. A bright line of stinging pain.

I gasped. They clattered onto the counter, too loud in the quiet room.

I froze, staring at the door. Blood welled from the cut, warm and slick. I waited.

No movement.

Twenty-one. Twenty-two.

Snatch the scissors up. Saw harder. Ignore the blood. Ignore the pain.

Snap.

The tie fell away.

I ripped it off and rubbed the circulation back into my hands, staring at the red grooves left behind. My skin was angry and abraded, but my hands were mine.

Forty-six.

I looked at the door, then at my feet.

He hadn't tied my ankles. He hadn't even tied me to the bed frame.

Stupid man, I thought. *Arrogant man.*

But was it stupidity? Or something else? He was the Enforcer, the one who watched everything, who missed nothing. He had tied my hands in front of me; a beginner's mistake, one that ensured I could reach the drawer, find the scissors, cut myself free.

Maybe he wanted me to.

The thought lingered for a heartbeat longer than it should have.

Maybe he's tired of the cage too.

No. That was the kind of thinking that got people killed. He had been brought to the compound as a child and raised inside its bones, and his whole life had been spent keeping people exactly where the leader wanted them. I was no different from any of the others he'd dragged back.

I flicked it away hard and didn't let it come back.

Fifty-two. Fifty-three.

I grabbed the plastic bag, shoved the book and the scissors inside, and crawled out the bathroom window.

The fall was harder than I expected. I landed in a crouch on the concrete, my ankles screaming in protest.

But I was out.

I ran.

* * * *

I didn't stop running for two days.

It was a blur of grey highway shoulders and dense treacherous woods. I moved at night, hiding in brambles and ditches during the daylight hours, sleeping in increments so short they barely counted as sleep at all.

The first night I ran until my lungs felt like they'd been scraped raw. My feet, still tender from the river, screamed with every step, the blisters splitting open and bleeding into my socks. But I couldn't stop. Wouldn't stop. Every mile was a victory. Every hour that passed without seeing his car in the distance was proof I might actually make it.

I stole water from garden hoses, the metallic taste coating my throat with every swallow. I ate stale crackers from a gas station dumpster I raided while the clerk's back was turned, the food sitting like concrete in my empty stomach. I'd never stolen food before. Never had to. In the compound there had always been meals, simple as they were. In my mother's apartment there had at least been cereal and ramen.

This was different. This was survival stripped down to its bones.

Fear was a constant companion, a cold weight sitting on my chest. Every snapping twig was a footstep. Every pair of headlights in the distance was his car. Every shadow at the edge of my vision was him; tall, broad-shouldered, inevitable. I felt watched constantly, as if the points of the compass had been painted on the back of my neck.

I slept in fits and starts, jolting awake at the sound of wind, and in the moments between sleeping and waking his voice was always there. *Got yourself caught because of a story.* In my dreams he was always just behind me, arms crossed, watching me run with that patient amusement, like he already knew where I was going before I did. I'd wake gasping and have to remind myself; just a dream, just paranoia, he can't find you.

The fear didn't listen to logic.

By the second night my body was a symphony of aches. Every muscle protested. My hair was matted with dirt and sweat. I developed a pattern without deciding to; walk until my legs buckled, find somewhere to hide, sleep in twenty-minute increments, wake, move again. Behind a dumpster. In an abandoned shed. Once in a drainage culvert with water running cold over my ankles.

Prey behaviour. I was learning to think like something hunted.

I managed to get on a city bus, huddled in the back seat with my hood pulled low, watching every face that boarded at every stop. The bus was warm, too warm after the cold nights, and I had to fight to keep my eyes open. I switched three times, changing my clothes in a public restroom at one of the depots, washing the dirt from my face and forcing my expression into something neutral in the mirror.

My reflection stared back at me; gaunt, haunted, eyes too wide and skin too pale.

I looked like prey.

I pulled my hair into a ponytail, splashed water on my face, and told myself I just looked tired. Tired was invisible. Tired was everyone on a Greyhound heading west.

I bought a ticket with the last of my cash and found a window seat near the back and watched the buildings blur past the glass. Around me the bus filled with ordinary people living ordinary lives; an elderly woman with a crossword, a businessman on his phone, a young mother juggling a toddler and a nappy bag. Normal. All of it blindingly, beautifully normal.

I pressed my forehead against the cold glass and let out a long slow breath.

For the first time in forty-eight hours, I let my guard down. Just a fraction. Just enough to close my eyes and feel the hum of the engine through the seat and tell myself it was over.

I almost believed it.

CHAPTER 15

Freya

I let my head rest against the cold glass. The vibration of the engine hummed through my skull, almost soothing. Almost safe. I was miles away. I was in a moving vehicle. He couldn't track a bus. He couldn't be everywhere.

Could he?

No. That was paranoia talking. He was good, but he wasn't omniscient. The compound's reach was long, but it wasn't infinite.

I had almost convinced myself when exhaustion finally won. My eyes drifted closed, just for a second, letting the weight of two sleepless days pull at me.

The bus stopped at a depot on the edge of a small town.

A few people got off. A few got on.

I didn't look up. I kept my eyes on the tree line rushing past, trying to stay awake, trying to stay vigilant.

The seat next to me dipped under the weight of a new passenger.

I stiffened, instinctively pulling my backpack tighter, but I didn't look. I just wanted them to leave me alone. I just wanted to be invisible.

The new passenger settled in. I could feel their presence, too close in the cramped space. They smelled like soap. Clean. Out of place among the stale bus odours.

Wrong. Something about it felt wrong.

My pulse quickened.

"You know," a voice said, low and intimately familiar, "for someone who hates flying, you certainly cover a lot of ground."

My heart stopped.

The blood drained from my face so fast my vision swam. I knew that voice. I knew the cadence, the taunt.

No. No, no, no.

I turned my head slowly, dread coiling in my stomach like a snake.

It was him.

He was wearing a baseball cap pulled low, shadowing his face, but I could see the hard set of his jaw, the slope of his nose. He was leaning back, relaxed, one arm draped along the back of the seat behind me. Casual. Like we were old friends catching up. Like he hadn't just hunted me across three states.

He looked at me, his eyes dark and amused.

Not angry. Not frustrated. Amused. Like this was a game. Like I was entertainment.

"You're a hard girl to find, Freya," he said softly. "But you're predictable."

I opened my mouth to scream, to shove him, to do anything, but he shifted. Something hard and cold jammed into my ribs, hidden under the fold of his jacket between our bodies.

A gun.

The world tilted. My stomach dropped. All the air left my lungs in a rush.

"Don't make a scene," he murmured, leaning in closer, his breath warm against my ear. "You know how much I dislike scenes."

The bus lurched forward, merging onto the highway. The chatter of the other passengers, the drone of the engine, all of it horrifically normal. While my world was ending again, right here in seat 24B.

He pressed the gun harder into my side, a warning, a promise.

"Hello again, my little bird," he murmured, his eyes crinkling with that terrifying not-quite smile. His free hand reached over and plucked my backpack from my lap with infuriating ease. He set it on the floor between his feet, claiming it. Claiming me.

"Did you really think you could outrun me?" he asked, his voice barely above a whisper. "I've been following you since the motel. Every bus. Every stop. You ran in circles, Freya."

The realisation hit like a physical blow. He'd been tracking me the entire time. Watching. Waiting. Letting me exhaust myself. He'd seen me steal water. Seen me sleep in ditches. Seen me change my clothes in that bathroom. He'd been there the whole time, always three steps behind, letting me think I was free.

The cruelty of it made me want to vomit.

"I could have taken you a dozen times," he continued, his voice conversational, like we were discussing the weather. "The drainage culvert on Highway 12. The gas station bathroom in Millbrook. The abandoned shed behind the church. But I wanted to see how far you'd run. How resourceful you'd be."

Each location was a knife in my gut.

"You did better than I expected," he said, and there was almost a note of approval in his voice. "Most runaways panic. Make stupid mistakes. You kept your head. Mostly."

"You're hurting me," I hissed, keeping my eyes fixed on the seat in front of me.

"Good," he said softly. "Pain is a great teacher. It keeps you present."

"How did you find me?" The words came out in a rush. "I was careful. I paid cash. I didn't use my name."

He laughed, low and humourless, the sound vibrating against my shoulder.

"You were careful like a child is careful, Freya. You were terrified. Terrified people leave trails a mile wide. You think paying cash hides you? You think jumping on a bus makes you invisible?"

"I was gone," I insisted.

"You were exactly where I expected you to be. Running blind. And you're loud, little bird. You panic in crowds. You flinch at shadows. You shine like a beacon in the dark."

Little bird.

He'd called me that before, in the motel room. It was condescending, possessive, and yet it also felt oddly intimate. Like he saw me. Really saw me, in a way no one at the compound ever had. I shook my head, disgusted with myself. He didn't see me. He saw a runaway to retrieve, a problem to solve. That was all.

The bus hit a pothole, the suspension bouncing violently. The gun dug in again, sharp and agonising.

"Stop moving," Andre warned, his voice dropping an octave. "Or I'll make this a lot worse than a bruise."

I froze, forcing myself to breathe through the pain.

We drove for what felt like an eternity. I watched the scenery change from city outskirts to industrial lots, the grey light deepening into twilight. *Please let someone notice,* I prayed silently. *Please let the driver look in the mirror.*

No one looked. The world was indifferent to my abduction.

"Where are you taking me?" I asked, my voice trembling.

"Home," he said simply.

"I don't have a home."

"You do now."

The bus began to slow, the brakes hissing. We were pulling into a depot on the edge of a town I didn't recognise.

"Stand up," Andre ordered. "Slowly. Keep your hands in your lap."

My legs felt like lead, but I obeyed. He kept the gun hidden under the fold of his jacket, the threat absolute. He stood with me, his body blocking the aisle, a wall between me and the rest of the world.

He marched me down the aisle, every step a nightmare. I expected someone to notice, to scream, to stop us. The passengers just kept looking at their phones, exhausted and indifferent. We stepped off the bus into the grey light, the air cold and smelling of diesel. The doors hissed shut behind us.

"Don't try to run," Andre said, his grip tightening on my elbow as he steered me toward the parking lot.

I looked up at him, hating the calm authority in his eyes, the way he looked at me like I was a puzzle he had already solved. And hating that I was looking. Really looking. At the sharp line of his jaw, the way his dark hair fell across his forehead, the scar that cut through his left eyebrow.

At the compound I'd only ever seen him from a distance. Up close he was unsettling in a different way.

Handsome, a small voice whispered. *He's handsome, and that's why you keep noticing.*

I crushed the thought immediately. Handsome or not, he was dragging me back to hell.

"I hate you."

"I know," he said, guiding me toward a sedan parked under a flickering streetlight. "But you're coming with me anyway."

He opened the rear door and before I could climb in he caught my arm.

"Try to run," he said, his eyes locking onto mine, "and I won't just bring you back. I'll break you before we even cross the state line."

He put me in the backseat. The door slammed shut, the lock clicking with a finality that made my stomach drop.

* * * *

For the first hour of the drive I stared out the window, watching the miles disappear beneath the tyres. We were heading back. Back to the fences, the gardens, the prayer hall. Back to Him.

I hated Andre. I hated his easy posture, the way he lounged in the driver's seat like he was taking a Sunday drive. But mostly I hated how aware I was of him. Every time he shifted gears I noticed the flex of his forearm. Every time he checked the mirror his eyes would flick to mine for just a fraction of a second, and my breath would catch.

It was irrational. Insane. He'd taken me at gunpoint. He was driving me back to Father Michael, to the reintegration sessions I'd heard whispered about in the cabins. And yet my body kept reacting to him in ways I couldn't control. I didn't understand it. I didn't want to understand it. I pressed my forehead against the cool window glass, squeezed my eyes shut, and told myself it was just my mind trying to survive, reaching for something to hold onto in the dark.

It didn't help.

"You're too close," I snapped, unable to take the silence anymore. "Can't you just drive?"

He glanced at me in the rearview mirror, his expression unreadable.

"I'm driving, Freya. You're the one hyperventilating in the back seat."

"I'm not hyperventilating," I lied. "I'm trapped. You're taking me back to that prison."

"It's not a prison," he said, his voice maddeningly even. "It's the only place you can survive. Look at you. You were eating out of a dumpster two days ago. You were sleeping in a motel that rents by the hour."

"I was free!" I leaned forward against the barrier between the seats. "I belonged to myself. You can't just own people, Andre. It doesn't work like that."

He didn't even blink.

"You belong to the family. You belong to the

leader. And right now, you belong to me."

The way he said it sent a jolt through me that was equal parts fury and something else. Something hot and unwanted that coiled low in my belly.

I slumped back against the seat and wrapped my arms around myself and said nothing, because there was nothing to say that wouldn't make it worse.

* * * *

We stopped at a roadside diner as the sun began to set. The air was biting when we got out.

"Stay close," Andre said, falling into step beside me.

"I don't take orders from you," I muttered, veering toward the edge of the parking lot. I needed space. I needed to breathe air he hadn't already claimed.

He was faster than me.

Before I could take more than two steps he was there, blocking my path, using his larger frame to back me up against the rough brick wall of the diner. He didn't touch me. He just crowded me.

The sudden proximity was overwhelming. He smelled like pine needles and gasoline and something distinctly male, and I hated that I noticed. I could feel the heat radiating off his body, see the way his chest rose and fell. This close I could see the flecks of gold in his dark eyes, the scar through his left eyebrow, the stubble along his jaw.

Why was my brain cataloguing these details like they mattered?

"I told you to stay close," he said, his voice dipping into that register that did things to my knees I refused to acknowledge.

"I'm not a dog," I spat, tilting my chin up to meet his gaze. "I'm a human being."

"You're a flight risk," he corrected.

He braced a hand on the wall beside my head, caging me in without touching me. The heat of his body seeped into my skin anyway.

"And you're terrified."

"I'm not terrified of you," I lied.

"You should be," he murmured, his eyes dropping to my lips for just a second, then back to mine. The look was heavy, loaded with something I couldn't name. For one insane, terrifying second I thought he might close the distance. For one insane, terrifying second I thought I might let him.

"But I think you're terrified of yourself, too."

I froze. My breath caught in my throat.

He saw it. He saw the way my body had betrayed me, the confusion, the shame. And worse; he understood it.

"Get out of my way," I whispered.

He held my gaze for a heartbeat longer, searching my face. Then he stepped back, and the rush of cold air between us was like a slap.

"Fine," he said, his voice rough. "Let's eat."

He turned and walked into the diner, leaving me against the wall with my heart pounding a rhythm of fear and something I refused to name.

I stayed there for a moment. Trying to steady my breathing. Trying to make sense of what had just happened.

Nothing had happened. He'd crowded me, said something cutting, and walked away. That was all.

So why did the air still feel charged? Why did it feel like something had shifted in a way I couldn't put back?

I hated him.

I hated the compound.

But as I pushed off the wall and followed him inside, I knew with a sinking feeling that the walls of my cage were already changing shape.

CHAPTER 16

Andre

Day two blurred into a haze of asphalt and grey skies.

The obsession was a low hum in my blood, constant and distracting. I watched her. I couldn't help it. In the passenger seat now instead of the back, she was a constant presence in my periphery. The way she twisted her hands in her lap when she was nervous. The way she stared out the window as if the landscape itself might offer her an escape route.

The air in the car was thick, heavy with two days of silence. Freya's knees were pulled up to her chest, a physical barrier between us. She shifted restlessly, rubbing her arms.

"Can you turn the heat on? It's freezing."

I didn't take my eyes off the road.

"I'm comfortable."

"Well, I'm not," she snapped. "My fingers are

numb."

"Put on your jacket."

She let out a frustrated huff and reached for the radio dial instead, spinning the knob aggressively away from the static-filled country station I'd been listening to. The noise shifted to a blaring, rhythmic pop song.

"I hate that music," she said, glaring at the dashboard. "It's depressing."

"And I hate you touching the controls," I countered.

I reached out, covering her hand with mine and forcing the dial back. My skin was hot against hers, and for a second neither of us moved. She snatched her hand away as if I'd burned her, cradling it against her chest.

"You're impossible," she muttered, sinking back into the seat.

"And you're a passenger, Freya. Passengers don't pick the playlist."

My throat was dry, the road stretching endlessly ahead. Without signalling my intent I leaned across her lap to the glove box. The space in the cab was tight. As I reached across her my arm brushed against her chest; not a grab, not deliberate, just the friction of movement in a confined space. But she froze. Her breath hitched, a sharp audible intake that seemed to suck the oxygen out of the car. She didn't pull away immediately. She just tensed, her muscles locking up, her head turning toward the window as if to hide the flush rising on her neck.

"You're suffocating me," she whispered, her voice tight.

I grabbed the bottle and pulled back. The scent of her, rain and pine and that specific electric smell of her skin, lingered on my sleeve.

"Stop breathing my air then," I shot back, my voice sharper than I intended.

The words hung there, heavy and loaded. The physical attraction was instant, constant, and unwelcome. It threaded through our clashes, turning every grip and shove into something charged. I could feel it radiating off her, a mix of fear and fascination. I glanced over. She was looking back at me now, her eyes wide and defiant, refusing to back down. She didn't see an enforcer right then. She looked at me like I was actually a man, not just an instrument. It was a disarming gaze. She saw the monster, but she also saw the man holding the leash.

It sent a thrill through me like nothing else ever had.

I took a swig of water and dropped the bottle in the cupholder and tightened my grip on the steering wheel until my knuckles turned white, forcing myself to look back at the road, terrified of what I might do if I kept looking at her.

* * * *

We stopped at a gas station mid-day. While I pumped gas she stood by the car, arms crossed, shivering in the wind.

"You look like a ghost," I said, leaning against the pump.

"And you look like a jailer," she shot back. But there was a tremor in her voice. "I don't understand how you don't see it, Andre. The emptiness. The way they look at Father Michael like he's a god."

I capped the tank and stepped into her space, backing her against the car door until she had nowhere to go. She froze, her eyes wide.

"He is a god," I said, my voice calm. Calmer than ice. "He saved us. You think you know the world? You know nothing. My mother, before the compound, she was nothing. She was less than nothing. She was drowning in filth and alcohol and men who used her up until there was nothing left."

Freya's anger faltered. She looked up at me, searching my face.

"And that justifies locking people up? It justifies breaking them?"

"It justifies order," I said. "It justifies purpose."

"I have purpose," she whispered, her defiance desperate but undercut by a raw honesty. "I have my own purpose."

"Not anymore," I said. "Now, you have me."

* * * *

That night, in another nondescript motel room, the tension finally snapped.

I didn't plan it. The air was thick with the

scent of her fear and the lingering adrenaline of the road. She tried to push past me to get to the bathroom and I caught her wrist. Her skin was warm under my fingers, her pulse racing like a trapped animal's. I yanked her back against my chest, feeling the sharp intake of her breath as her body collided with mine.

"Let go, Andre," Freya hissed, twisting in my grip, her eyes flashing with that familiar fire.

But there was something else there now; fear laced with heat, the kind that had been building since we hit the road.

"No, little bird," I murmured, my voice low and rough against her ear.

I spun her around to face me, pinning her wrists above her head against the motel wall with one hand. The other slid to her throat, not squeezing, just holding her there, feeling her swallow hard. "You're not running from this. Not from me."

She bucked against me, her knee coming up toward my groin, but I shifted just in time, pressing my thigh between her legs to trap her.

"Stop it," she gasped, but her hips twitched involuntarily, grinding against the pressure. Her cheeks flushed, betraying her.

I leaned in closer, my lips brushing her jaw. "Your mouth says stop, but your body's begging for more. Feel that?"

I rocked my thigh harder, watching her eyes widen as friction hit her core through her thin pants. She bit her lip, stifling a whimper.

"I hate you," she whispered, but it came out shaky, her breath hitching.

"Good," I said, releasing her wrists only to grab the hem of her shirt and rip it upward. The fabric tore easily, exposing her breasts. Her nipples hardened in the cool air.

"Hate me all you want, little bird. But you're mine tonight."

Freya's hands came up to push me away, but I caught them again, twisting a nearby lamp cord from the nightstand and using it to bind her wrists together behind her back. She struggled, cursing under her breath, but I tied it tight, the knots biting into her skin just enough to leave marks.

"What the fuck are you doing? Untie me!"

Her voice cracked, panic edging in, but I saw the way her thighs clenched together. I ignored her, shoving her down onto the bed face-first. She landed with a muffled yelp, her bound hands trapped beneath her. I straddled her hips, my weight pinning her as I yanked her pants and panties down in one rough pull, leaving her bare and exposed. Her pussy was already slick, glistening in the dim light, and I couldn't resist running my fingers along her slit, teasing her folds.

"Look at you," I growled, dipping one finger inside her, just enough to feel her clench around it. She moaned despite herself, her hips lifting slightly. "So wet for the man who's tying you up.

You like this, don't you? Being helpless."

"No," she lied, her face buried in the pillow, but her body arched back toward my hand.

I added a second finger, thrusting deeper, curling them to hit that spot that made her gasp. Her walls fluttered, sucking me in, and I pumped slowly, building the rhythm while my thumb circled her clit.

"Liar," I said, leaning down to bite her shoulder, not hard enough to break skin, but enough to sting.

She cried out, a mix of pain and pleasure, her pussy tightening around my fingers.

"Tell me to stop, then. Say it like you mean it."

"Stop... please," she whimpered, but it was weak, her breath coming in pants as I fingered her harder, my palm slapping against her ass with each thrust.

I pulled my fingers out abruptly. She whined at the loss, her hips bucking for more.

"See? Your pussy's weeping for it. But we're just getting started."

I reached into my pocket for the knife I'd been carrying since the motel in Millbrook; sharp, familiar, a tool I knew how to use carefully. I flipped it open, the blade catching the light, and Freya froze beneath me, her body going rigid.

"Andre... what, don't," she breathed, twisting her head to look back at me, eyes wide with terror.

"Shh, little bird," I said, my free hand stroking her back. "I'm not going to hurt you. Much."

I trailed the flat of the blade along her spine, cool metal kissing her skin, watching goosebumps rise. She shivered, a soft sob escaping her lips. Slowly I pressed the edge against the curve of her ass cheek, just enough to prick, a tiny bead of blood welling up. She gasped, pain flashing across her face, but I followed it with my mouth, licking the spot clean, sucking gently until she moaned.

"It hurts," she protested, but her voice was breathy, needy.

"And it feels good too, doesn't it?"

I nicked her other cheek lightly, then soothed it with my tongue, the metallic tang mixing with her skin. My fingers returned to her pussy, sliding in easily now, fucking her with three digits while the knife danced along her thighs; teasing, threatening, never cutting deep.

"Fuck... Andre," she panted, her bound hands flexing uselessly. "Why are you doing this?"

"Because I want you to feel everything," I said, my voice husky. "Every sting, every touch. Every time you fight it and lose."

I flipped her over roughly, her back hitting the mattress, wrists still tied. I dragged the knife's tip between her breasts, light as a whisper, circling one nipple until it beaded harder. Then I leaned down and took it in my mouth, sucking hard while the blade pressed just enough to dimple the skin without breaking it. She arched into me, crying out, her legs spreading wide.

"I don't want this," she whispered, hating herself for the way her body responded. I could tell.

"Your nipples disagree," I said against her skin, switching to the other, biting down sharply before licking away the ache.

My fingers plunged back into her pussy, scissoring inside her, stretching her while my thumb ground her clit. She was soaking my hand, her juices dripping down to her ass.

"I shouldn't... oh god," she moaned, her head thrashing.

I set the knife aside, grabbing her thighs and spreading them wider.

"Look at me, little bird."

Her eyes met mine, hazy with lust and conflict. I lowered my head, my tongue flicking out to taste her; salty, sweet, all hers. I lapped at her folds, sucking her clit into my mouth, grazing it with my teeth just enough to make her yelp.

"Too much," she gasped, but her hips rolled up, fucking my face.

"Not enough," I growled, shoving my tongue inside her, fucking her with it while my fingers dug into her thighs, nails leaving crescents. I alternated; tongue thrusting deep, then pulling back to circle her clit, nipping lightly. Her breaths came in sobs, pleasure overriding the pain from the earlier pricks.

"Andre... I'm—"

She cut off with a scream as I sucked harder, my fingers joining in again, curling relentlessly.

"Come for me," I commanded, my voice muffled against her pussy. "Show me how much you need this."

She shattered, her body convulsing, pussy clenching around my fingers as she squirted a little, wetting my chin. I didn't stop, licking her through it, drawing out every tremor until she was begging me to stop for real this time.

I rose up, wiping my mouth. My cock was straining against my pants, but I wouldn't fuck her. Not yet. I unbound her wrists just to flip her onto her stomach again, retying them to the headboard with the cord extended.

"What now?" she panted, exhausted but still quivering.

"Now, you feel me, without me inside you," I said, picking up the knife once more. I traced it down her spine, then between her ass cheeks, pressing the handle; smooth, cool, against her tight hole. Not entering, just teasing, vibrating it lightly as I fingered her pussy from behind.

"No... that's, ah!"

She bucked as I pinched her clit, the pain sparking fresh pleasure.

"Your ass is clenching for it," I said, my free hand spanking her hard, leaving a red handprint over the tiny cut. "Admit it, little bird. Your body craves the hurt."

"I don't... I hate this," she finally spat, her voice small but defiant, even as her pussy gushed around my fingers. "You're sick."

Words spilled from us, her denials mixing with my taunts, her protests warring with her involuntary moans, until she came again, harder, her body a trembling mess against her will.

When it was over she lay curled on the bed, trembling, looking at me with a mix of hatred and devastation.

* * * *

The next day was quieter.

The dynamic between us had shifted. The fighting was still there, but it was laced with a heavy unspoken knowledge. She was terrified of me, yes. But she was also undeniably bound to me now. We drove through the afternoon, the silence stretching until it was almost comfortable. The attraction was a live wire between us, humming beneath the surface. Every time I shifted gears I saw her pulse jump in her throat. Every time she looked at me I saw the memory of the night before in her eyes.

We stopped at a diner that was a relic of the interstate, a chrome and neon oasis in the middle of nowhere that smelled of burnt coffee and bleach. We slid into a booth near the back, the vinyl sticking to my jeans. Freya sat opposite me, her hood pulled low, her gaze darting around the room like a trapped bird.

The waitress appeared, a woman with tired eyes and a stain on her apron. She slammed a mug of black coffee in front of me without a word, the liquid sloshing over the rim.

"And for you?" she barked at Freya, tapping her pen against her pad.

"Um... water, please," Freya whispered, shrinking slightly. "And... could I get some sugar?"

The waitress huffed, rolling her eyes.

"We're not a full service restaurant, honey. If you want sugar, it's on the counter."

She turned on her heel and walked away, leaving us in a cloud of cheap perfume and hostility. Freya shrank into her coat, pulling the fabric tight around her chin. She stared at the tabletop, tracing the scratches in the Formica, making herself as small as possible.

It was a familiar posture. The girl who didn't matter. The girl who didn't take up space. The compound had trained her well, but the world was reinforcing the lesson.

I watched her, a cold anger settling in my gut. I was used to people being afraid of me, or avoiding me. I was an enforcer. But seeing her dismissed, treated like nothing by a woman who didn't know she was running for her life, it grated on nerves I didn't know I still had.

I looked at the empty booth beside us. A glass sugar dispenser sat there, gathering dust. I reached over, my arm stretching across the aisle, and placed it gently in front of her. The glass clinked softly against her mug.

"Here," I said.

She looked up, startled. The hood slipped back, revealing her face. Her fingers brushed mine as she reached for the glass; a fleeting electric contact that made her breath hitch. She didn't pull away immediately. For a second her eyes softened, the walls dropping just enough to show me the girl who loved stories about lions and wardrobes. The girl who had fought a river and a fence to be free.

"Thank you," she whispered, her voice rough.

"Eat," I grunted, turning back to my coffee to hide the sudden tightness in my chest. "Order something."

She looked down at the menu, her thumb rubbing over the corner of the plastic sleeve. I didn't pull my hand away immediately. I let it rest on the table near hers, my fingers curled loosely against the sticky surface.

A silent offer of protection in a world I knew was cruel.

CHAPTER 17

Freya

The grey light of dawn crept over the highway, and a shame so heavy it felt like a stone sitting on my chest.

I curled into the passenger seat, pulling my knees up, trying to hide from the memories of two nights ago. My body ached; a dull throbbing reminder of Andre's hands, his voice, the things he had done to me. The things he had made me feel. I felt sick with myself. I kept trying to deny that I had wanted it, that I had enjoyed it, but the evidence was written in the way my skin still hummed at the memory of his touch.

When he spoke, that low dominant cadence that brokered no argument, my pulse spiked. When he used his strength to corner me, to control me, a dark traitorous heat unfurled low in my belly. When he used that knife, I didn't expect to feel pleasure where I should have felt pain.

It was wrong. I knew it was wrong. He was the enemy. He was the one dragging me back to the hell I had escaped. But the line between fear and arousal had been blurred by the cult long before he met me. The cult had used submission and pain as weapons, teaching us that obedience was the highest form of love. Andre was weaponising those same instincts, twisting them into something that felt terrifyingly like intimacy. I had no language for the difference between violation and chosen intensity. I only knew that when he hurt me, I didn't feel broken. I felt seen.

He was redefining pain into pleasure.

I faced a new prison now. Not the compound itself, though that loomed closer with every mile; we were still three days away. But the man in the driver's seat. He was the bars of my cage.

Around midday we stopped at a busy travel plaza. I needed air. I needed to feel like a human being, not a possession.

"I need to use the restroom," I said, not looking at him.

Andre checked his watch.

"You have three minutes. If you're not at the door, I'll come looking."

"I know the drill," I snapped.

I walked into the crowded restroom, my heart hammering. There was a window near the sinks, high up but cracked open. I didn't think. I just moved. I climbed onto the counter, my sneakers slipping on the granite, and shoved the window up. I scrambled out, dropping into the alley behind the plaza.

My adrenaline spiked. I could see the interstate from here. I could flag down a trucker. I could disappear.

I ran toward the fence that separated the lot from the access road. I was almost there, my fingers brushing the chain-link, when a hand clamped around the back of my neck.

I didn't even hear him approach.

"Going somewhere?" He slammed me against the fence, the metal digging into my cheek.

I gasped, the breath knocked out of me. He didn't yell. He was terrifyingly calm.

"Let me go!" I clawed at his hand, kicking back at his shins.

"You have three seconds to stop fighting," he whispered in my ear. "Or I take you right here against this fence where everyone can see."

I froze, humiliation washing over me.

"I hate you."

"No, you don't," he said, his grip tightening, steering me back toward the car in the shadow of the building. "You just hate that you're mine."

He shoved me into the backseat and slid in after me, locking the doors. The tinted windows hid us from the passing families, the truckers, the world. The air smelled of stale smoke and car freshener, but all I could focus on was the heat of his body pressing me into the seat as he shoved me face-down.

"You're going to learn, little bird," he growled, yanking my wrists behind my back and securing them with a zip tie.

I twisted, trying to pull free, but he just laughed, a dark sound that sent shivers down my spine.

"Let me go, Andre. This is fucked up," I spat, my cheek pressed against the scratchy fabric, heart pounding.

But even as I said it my pussy clenched, a traitorous ache building between my legs.

He didn't answer with words. His palm cracked against my ass, the sting blooming hot and sharp. I yelped, bucking up, but he held me down with one hand on my lower back, the other stripping my pants and panties off in a swift brutal motion. Cool air hit my bare skin, and I felt exposed, vulnerable, my slick folds already betraying me.

"Look at that," he murmured, fingers tracing my slit, dipping just inside to feel how wet I was. "Your cunt's dripping. You say no, but this says yes."

"No," I whispered fiercely, shaking my head, even as my hips twitched toward his touch. "I don't want you. I hate this."

His finger slid deeper, curling inside me, stroking that spot that made my toes curl. I bit my lip to stifle the moan, but it escaped anyway, humiliating me further.

"Liar," he said, adding a second finger, thrusting slow and deep, his thumb pressing my clit in firm circles.

The pressure built, pleasure coiling tight despite the burn in my wrists from the ties. He spanked me again, harder, the slap echoing, leaving my skin throbbing. Pain flared, mixing with the heat in my core, making everything sharper, more intense.

"You will stop running, little bird."

"Stop," I gasped, but it came out breathy, broken, as his fingers pumped faster, scissoring to stretch me.

My walls fluttered around him, sucking him in, and I hated how good it felt, how my body arched back for more.

"Please... it's too much. You're deranged."

He pulled his fingers out suddenly and I whimpered at the emptiness, cursing myself for it. Then I heard it; the unmistakable click of him drawing his gun. My blood ran cold.

"Andre, no. Don't you dare," I pleaded, twisting to look at him over my shoulder, eyes wide with real fear.

"Shh," he soothed, but there was no gentleness in his eyes. Just possession.

He flipped me onto my back, my bound hands trapped under me, pulling my shoulders taut. The gun's barrel was cold against my thigh as he traced it up, the metal sending goosebumps racing across my skin.

"I'm not going to shoot you, little bird. But you'll feel this. Every inch of control I have over you."

He pressed the flat side of the barrel to my inner thigh, sliding it higher, teasing the edge of my folds without entering. I squeezed my legs together but he forced them apart with his knee, his free hand pulling one ankle up and pinning it, leaving me near immobile.

"Open up," he commanded, and when I shook my head he slapped my pussy, light but stinging, making me cry out.

"Fuck you," I hissed, tears pricking my eyes, but my clit throbbed from the impact, swelling under his gaze.

He flipped the gun so the handle; smooth, thick, unyielding, nudged against my entrance.

"This'll fill you just right. It's no cock, but you'll take it anyway."

"No, Andre, please," I begged, even as my hips lifted slightly, my body craving the stretch.

He pushed the handle in slowly, inch by inch, the cool hardness invading me, pressing against my walls. It wasn't him, but it was him; his weapon, his power. The thought made my stomach twist with shame and heat. I clenched around it, a sob escaping as he twisted it gently, angling to hit deep.

"That's it," he murmured, his mouth descending to my breast, sucking my nipple hard. His teeth grazed it, biting just enough to hurt, sending jolts straight to my core.

The handle thrust in and out now, shallow at first, then deeper, his grip steady and unrelenting.

"Your pussy's gripping it like a vice. You love being stuffed like this, don't you?"

"I don't," I lied, my voice cracking as pleasure built, coiling tighter with each push. My thighs trembled, slickness coating the handle, easing the way. He leaned down again, his tongue flicking my other nipple before nipping sharply. Pain sparked, blending with the fullness inside me, making my back arch. His thumb found my clit, rubbing in tight circles.

"Say it again," he taunted, speeding up the thrusts. "Tell me you hate it while you come undone."

"I hate you," I moaned, head thrashing, but my body was on fire, chasing the edge.

He spanked my inner thigh, the crack loud in the car, then soothed it with his mouth, sucking the skin until I whimpered. The dual sensations, pain blooming and fading into pleasure, pushed me closer, my breaths coming in ragged gasps.

He dropped the gun then, leaving me empty and aching, but replaced it with his fingers; three now, plunging deep, curling relentlessly while his mouth moved lower. His tongue lapped at my clit, hot and insistent, sucking it between his lips as he fingered me harder.

"Come on, little bird," he growled against my

skin. "Show me how much your body needs this."

I shattered, screaming his name despite myself, my pussy spasming around his fingers, juices squirting out in hot bursts. Waves of ecstasy crashed over me, leaving me trembling, tears streaming down my face from the intensity and the betrayal of my own desires. He didn't stop, licking me through it, drawing out every aftershock until I was a boneless, sobbing mess.

"No more," I whispered finally, my voice hoarse, as he pulled away.

But even in the haze, the denial burned. I didn't want it. I couldn't want it. No matter what my body screamed.

"You will not run from me again," he warned, his voice quiet and absolute. "Or this will seem like child's play. Don't test me, little bird."

****

The afternoon bled out slowly around us.

He drove. I sat. Neither of us spoke and the silence had a texture to it, thick and close, like the air before a storm that never quite broke. I watched the landscape change through the window; flat scrubland giving way to low hills, the light going amber and then copper as the sun dropped toward the treeline. My wrists still ached where the zip tie had bitten. I pressed my thumb into the marks without thinking, the dull throb grounding me in a way I didn't want to examine.

I was aware of him the way you're aware of

a fire in a small room. Not looking at it directly. Just feeling the heat.

Once, he shifted gears and his forearm crossed into my peripheral vision, and I looked away before I could catch myself looking. I pressed my forehead against the cool glass and watched the white lines of the highway blur past and tried to remember what it had felt like to want to run. Three days ago I had been certain. Two days ago I had still been certain. Now the certainty had a crack running through it and I didn't know when that had happened or how to close it.

The sky turned grey. The hills flattened out again.

"You have to stop running, Freya," he said finally, his eyes on the road.

He sounded almost bored.

"I can't go back there," I whispered, staring at my hands. "You know what they do to people who run. They erase them."

"They won't erase you," he said. "I won't let them."

"You can't stop him," I said, my voice cracking. "You're his dog, Andre. You do what he says."

"Watch your mouth," he warned, but there was no heat in it.

We lapsed back into silence. Outside, the first motel signs began to appear at the roadside, their neon bleeding into the dusk. I watched them pass, one after another, and said nothing.

* * * *

That night we stopped at another motel. I was exhausted, my resolve fraying. But as he turned the key in the door I saw it; a fire alarm on the wall outside our room. It was a desperate, stupid chance, but I was drowning.

As he leaned over the bed to plug in his phone, I bolted, hitting the alarm and pulling the lever. The wail of the siren was deafening. People started shouting in the hallway. I used the chaos to slip out the door, merging with the confused crowd.

I made it to the stairwell.

I was halfway down, freedom tasting like copper in my mouth, when a hand shot out from the landing below.

Andre. He wasn't chasing me. He was waiting. He had known.

He grabbed my arm, jerking me off balance. I tumbled down the last few steps, crashing into him at the bottom. He caught me effortlessly, holding me up as my legs gave out.

"Did you really think that would work?" he asked, his voice steady despite the blaring siren. "That I would lose you in a crowd? I saw you look at the alarm."

"Let me go!" I screamed, hoping someone would hear. "Help! Fire!"

"Go back to your rooms," Andre barked at the gathering crowd, flashing a badge that looked official enough to make them hesitate. "Drunk girlfriend. Everything's under control."

The people drifted away, murmuring, annoyed but uninterested. The alarm was cut off by a manager down the hall. Silence rushed back in, heavy and suffocating.

Andre didn't waste a second. He hauled me up the stairs by my arm, his fingers bruising, dragging me back to the room without a word. The door slammed behind us, deadbolt clicking, chain rattling into place.

He turned then, his eyes dark across the dim space, the single lamp casting long shadows that made him look even larger, more inescapable.

He lunged, grabbing my throat with one hand and slamming me against the wall, the impact jarring my teeth.

"You think you can run from me, little bird?" he growled, his face inches from mine, breath hot and ragged. "I'll break that spirit if I have to."

"Fuck you," I spat, but fear coiled in my gut, mixing with the unwanted heat his touch always ignited.

He laughed, low and cruel, and shoved me onto the floor. I landed hard, hands scrabbling against the carpet as I tried to get away. But he was on me in an instant, straddling my thighs, his weight crushing the fight from my limbs. His hand cracked against my ass, the slap sharp and stinging, heat blooming across my skin. I yelped, bucking wildly, but he did it again, harder, each impact sending jolts through me that pooled low in my belly despite the pain.

"Stop! I hate you," I sobbed, tears pricking my eyes, but my pussy throbbed, slickness gathering between my thighs.

He ripped my pants down, exposing me. Fingers traced my slit from behind, dipping in to feel the wetness, and he hummed in approval.

"Your body's honest, even if your mouth isn't."

He flipped me onto my back, his knees bracketing my hips to hold me in place. He drew his pocket knife from his boot, the blade glinting in the low light. My breath hitched, fear spiking sharp.

"Andre, no. Please, don't. Not again."

"Shh," he murmured, pressing the flat of the blade to my collarbone, cool metal sliding down between my breasts.

He sliced my shirt open with deliberate care, the fabric parting without nicking skin, exposing my breasts. The tip pricked just above my nipple, a tiny sting that drew a bead of blood, and I gasped, arching involuntarily. He licked it away, tongue hot and rough, the sensation sending sparks straight to my core.

"See? Pain makes you feel alive," he whispered, trailing the knife lower, over my stomach, circling my navel before pressing it lightly to my inner thigh, carefully piercing the skin.

I squeezed my legs together but he forced them apart with his knee, moving the blade to tease along my folds without cutting, the threat alone making me clench.

"Beg me to stop, Freya. Or beg for more."

"Please," I whimpered, shaking my head, but my hips lifted toward the pressure, craving the edge.

He set the knife aside. His mouth descended, sucking one nipple hard, teeth grazing until it ached, biting down just enough to make me cry out. Pain flared, white-hot, but it twisted into pleasure as his hand slid between my legs, fingers plunging into my soaked pussy, thrusting deep and curling. I moaned despite myself, walls fluttering around him, the fullness overwhelming. He added a third finger, stretching me, pumping relentlessly while his thumb ground against my clit.

"That's it, little bird. Let it out."

The belt from his jeans whispered free of its loops; thick leather, worn and heavy. He looped it around my throat, the buckle cold against my skin, and pulled it snug. The pressure built like a vice, restricting my breath in slow deliberate increments. The world tilted as the air thinned, my chest heaving against the leather's grip. It wasn't just the loss of air; it was an unravelling, every denied gasp amplifying the sensations crashing through me. Colours bloomed behind my eyelids, red and gold, while my pulse thundered in my ears in sync with the curl of his fingers inside me. The lack of oxygen sharpened everything;

the rough drag of his knuckles against my inner walls, the insistent pressure on my swollen clit, the lingering sting from the knife's prick on my breast.

Pleasure coiled tighter, euphoric and terrifying, my body floating on the edge where pain dissolved into bliss, each shallow breath a spark that fed the fire building low in my core.

He tightened the belt with a sharp tug, my vision spotting with stars, and the euphoria deepened; weightless, like diving into warm endless waves. My lungs burned sweetly, every touch turning electric, my pussy clenching around his fingers as if chasing the air he stole.

"Look at you," he taunted, loosening just enough for me to rasp a breath before cinching it again. "Choking on my belt, soaking my hand. You love this edge, don't you?"

"I hate this," I gasped when he allowed air, tears streaming down my face, my hands pushing weakly at his chest. "You're a monster. Let me go."

But the words dissolved into a moan as he bit my other nipple, pain lancing through the haze, blending with the rush that made my skin hum.

"But you come so pretty for the monster," he taunted, tightening the belt once more as his fingers thrust harder, curling to hit that spot that made stars burst anew.

My body betrayed me utterly, thighs quaking, pussy spasming around his fingers as the orgasm ripped through me; a tidal wave that left me trembling, squirting against his palm in helpless pulses. He loosened the belt, the sudden rush of oxygen crashing like a drug, intensifying the aftershocks until I whimpered. Then he tightened it again, the cycle renewing the euphoria, that floating surrender where my mind blurred and every sensation amplified into overwhelming rapture. His tongue delved between my folds, lapping at my release while his fingers resumed their assault, sucking my clit with bruising force, the belt's grip turning the world into a kaleidoscope of bliss and burn.

I shattered a second time, sobbing his name in a broken plea, waves of ecstasy crashing over the pain, wringing me dry.

My body was limp and trembling beneath him. The euphoria faded as he finally released the belt, the rush of air leaving me dizzy, spent. I curled into myself on the floor, unable to move, muscles like water, tears soaking into the rough carpet. He stood over me, breathing heavy, but I couldn't look up, couldn't face the satisfaction in his eyes. The pain lingered, a dull throb, but worse was the afterglow; the shameful satisfaction my body clung to, even as my mind screamed in devastation.

Andre sat on the edge of the bed, looking down at me. He looked calm. Unruffled.

"Why do you keep trying to run?" he asked, his voice soft, dangerous. "You know I'm just going to catch you. You know I'm going to punish you."

I turned my head away, burying my face in my arms.

"Because I have to."

"Do you?" he persisted. "Or do you just like the punishment?"

"I don't," I lied.

"We both know otherwise, Freya. Your body sings for it."

"I'm not my body!" I shouted, rolling over to glare at him. "You're a monster."

He laughed, a low dark sound.

"I didn't force you to enjoy it, little bird. I just gave you permission to stop fighting yourself."

He stood and went into the bathroom. I heard the water running. When he came back out he had a wet washcloth. He knelt beside me on the floor. I flinched, expecting him to grab me. Instead, he gently wiped the tears from my face and the blood from my body.

The gesture was so tender, so at odds with the man who had just held a belt to my throat, that it broke something inside me.

"You're only making it worse for yourself," he said quietly. "We're a couple days out. Just... stop fighting. Let me take care of you."

"I can't," I whispered, leaning into his hand despite myself. "If I stop fighting, I'm gone."

He sighed, brushing a stray hair away from my forehead.

"You're not gone. You're right here. With me."

The words settled over me, heavy and terrifying. He was the cage. He was the key.

And the worst part was, I wasn't sure I wanted him to let me out anymore.

CHAPTER 18

Andre

The silence in the car was heavy, broken only by the ragged, wet sound of Freya's breathing.

I drove with one hand on the wheel, my eyes darting periodically to the passenger seat. She was curled in on herself, trying to make herself small. But every time the car hit a bump in the asphalt, she flinched, a sharp intake of breath that hissed through her teeth. Each flinch registered like a physical blow. I told myself it was annoyance. Damaged cargo complicated delivery. But that was a lie, and I was getting tired of lying to myself.

"You're in pain," I said. It wasn't a question.

"I'm fine," she whispered, not looking at me. She stared out the window at the passing surroundings, her reflection ghostly in the glass.

"You're bleeding on the upholstery."

I saw her glance down at her feet. She had kicked off her shoes miles back, unable to bear the pressure of leather against her skin. Her socks had dark stains spreading through the fabric.

Her escape through the river had cost her dearly. The rocks hadn't cared about her defiance. The current hadn't cared about her freedom.

I should have kept driving. Protocol said you didn't stop for injuries unless they were life-threatening. You delivered first, treated second. Father Michael didn't care for comfort stops.

But the thought of her bleeding quietly in that seat for another six hours made something twist in my gut.

"Next exit," I muttered, flicking on the blinker.

"I can keep going," she protested weakly as I pulled into the lot of a nondescript motel with a flickering vacancy sign. "Andre, please. Don't stop."

"Shut up, Freya."

I parked near the office, leaving the engine running while I went inside. I returned with a key in hand, dragging her out of the car.

Her legs buckled the moment her feet hit the pavement. She didn't scream; she just made a choked, broken sound and folded.

I caught her before she hit the ground.

I didn't think about it. Instinct took over.

"You should have told me it was this bad," I scolded.

I scooped her up, one arm behind her knees, the other around her back. She was lighter than she looked, all sharp angles and brittle bones.

Her weight in my arms felt significant. Not heavy; God, she was too light, probably hadn't eaten properly in days. But important. Like I was carrying something fragile that I couldn't afford to drop.

"You're heavy," I lied.

She didn't argue. She just turned her face into my chest, hiding from the neon lights that washed over us.

I felt her breath through my shirt. Warm. Alive. Trusting me not to drop her even though I'd given her every reason not to trust me at all.

I carried her to the room, kicked the door open, and laid her on the bed.

She scrambled backward immediately, pressing herself against the headboard, her eyes wide and terrified. She expected the chains. She expected zip ties. She expected the Enforcer to secure his prisoner.

"Sit," I ordered, nodding toward the bathroom.

She hesitated, her muscles coiled to run, but she saw the futility in my eyes. She limped into the small bathroom, sinking onto the closed lid of the toilet.

The room was cramped, smelling of bleach

and mildew. I retrieved the first aid kit from the car, a standard issue black bag I kept for field work. I set it on the counter and opened it. The click of the latches echoed in the small space.

"Feet," I said.

She flinched, pulling her feet under the hem of her dress.

"Andre..."

"Now." My voice was rough, but I kept it low. I wasn't shouting. I wasn't angry.

Slowly, painfully, she extended her left leg.

The sock was stuck to the dried blood. I had to peel it away. She hissed, her head falling back, tears squeezing from her eyes.

The skin was a mess. Abrasions covered her heels and soles, angry red patches of raw flesh, only at the beginning of healing. Some of the cuts were deep.

"River rocks," I said, kneeling on the tile floor in front of her. "They'll leave scars."

"I don't care," she breathed, her voice trembling.

But I cared. The realisation came swift and unwelcome. I cared that her feet would carry permanent marks from running. From me. From what I represented.

I cleaned a cloth with antiseptic from the kit.

"This will sting."

"I know."

I pressed the cloth to her heel. She jerked, her hand flying out to grab my shoulder. Her fingers dug into the muscle, hard enough to bruise, but I didn't pull away. I let her anchor herself to me.

It was the first time I had touched her without violence.

My hands, usually used to striking, to subduing, to dragging, were now moving with agonizing slowness. Careful. Gentle, even. Words I'd never associated with myself.

I wiped away the blood, revealing the raw damage beneath. Her skin was soft where it wasn't destroyed. Delicate. Human in a way that the hardened compound girls weren't anymore.

The enforcer mask slipped.

I looked at the wounds, and for the first time, I didn't see a defect in the system. I didn't see a runner who needed correction.

I saw what my devotion had cost her.

I was the chain around her neck. By proxy of the cult I served, I had chased her into this river. I had made these scars.

The guilt hit me, cold and suffocating.

I hated it. I hated the feeling of responsibility. I was a soldier. I was a weapon. Weapons didn't feel guilt for the impact.

But looking at her feet; at the evidence of what blind obedience cost, I felt a dark, unfamiliar heaviness in my chest.

This was necessary, I told myself. She needed to go back. She needed the structure, the safety. The outside world would destroy her.

But so would the compound. And I was the

instrument of that destruction either way.

"Does it look bad?" she whispered, her voice small.

"Raw," I said, my voice gruffer than usual to hide the tightening in my throat. "But you'll walk."

I moved to her other foot. She tried to pull it away, but I caught her ankle.

"Hold still."

She stilled, her breathing shallow. I cleaned this one with the same rough care. When I was done, I wrapped gauze around the soles, securing it with tape. It wasn't pretty, but it would protect the skin.

"Ribs," I said.

"Andre, please..."

"Lift your arms."

Reluctantly, she raised her arms. I lifted the hem of her dress.

The bruises on her side were already turning a deep, ugly purple, a map of the riverbank's violence. I touched the skin gently, probing for breaks.

Her skin was warm under my fingers. Softer than I expected. I could feel her heartbeat through the thin barrier of flesh and bone, rapid and frightened.

This was medical. Professional. But my body didn't seem to understand the distinction. I was hyperaware of every inch of exposed skin, the curve of her waist, the way she trembled under my touch.

Focus. You're checking for fractures, not—

She flinched, a sharp gasp escaping her lips.

But she didn't pull away from my hand. She leaned into the touch, her forehead dropping to rest against my shoulder.

It was a subtle movement, unconscious and desperate.

She wasn't flinching from the pain of my examination. She was flinching from the fear that I would stop caring. That terrified her more than the pain, that I would see the damage and discard her as broken goods.

And the fact that she was seeking comfort from me; from the man who'd tied her up, terrorized her, dragged her across state lines, spoke to just how isolated and desperate she really was.

I froze, my hand resting on the warm skin of her waist. Her forehead pressed into my shoulder, her breath hot against my collarbone. We were too close. This was too intimate for what we were supposed to be.

Captor and captive didn't lean on each other. They didn't seek comfort in the enemy's arms.

"I'm not going to break you, Freya," I said, the words coming out before I could stop them.

"You already have," she whispered against my shirt.

I pulled back slightly, looking down at her. Her eyes were red-rimmed, her face pale and exhausted. She looked at me with a mix of hatred and need that mirrored my own.

"I'm fixing it," I said firmly, wrapping an ace bandage around her ribs to support them. I pulled it tight, feeling the expansion of her lungs against my knuckles. "I fix what's mine."

The words hung between us, heavier than I'd intended. Not "I fix what I break." Not "I fix the compound's property."

Mine.

She heard it too. I saw the way her pupils dilated, the way her breath caught. She should have fought back, should have thrown the possessiveness in my face. But she didn't. She just looked at me with those wide, wounded eyes and nodded slightly.

Like she was accepting it. Like somewhere in the chaos of the last few days, she'd started to believe it too.

She didn't argue. She just watched me, her fingers tracing the hem of my sleeve where it rested near her face.

That touch; light, exploratory, almost tentative, did something to me. It wasn't sexual. It wasn't even really affectionate. It was seeking. Like she was trying to understand me through texture and proximity.

And I let her. Stood there like an idiot while this girl I'd hunted across three states traced the edge of my sleeve with her fingertips.

When I finished, I packed up the kit, but I didn't leave immediately. I knelt there on the bathroom floor, looking at the girl I had hunted, terrorized, and captured.

I had forced her back into the cage, but kneeling here on the cold tile, cleaning her wounds, I felt the bars of my own cage rattling.

"Go to bed," I said, standing up. My knee popped.

She reached out, her fingers brushing my wrist.

"Thank you," she whispered.

"Don't thank me," I snapped, turning away before she could see the conflict on my face. "I just need you to be able to move tomorrow."

I walked out of the bathroom, leaving the door open. I went and sat in the chair outside, next to the window.

I listened to her move, the rustle of sheets, the slow even out of her breathing as sleep finally took her.

I looked at my hands. They smelled of antiseptic and her skin.

I had spent years building walls to keep the guilt out, but tonight, looking at her bandaged feet, I realised I had opened a door I couldn't close.

She was injured, she was weak, and she was mine.

I wasn't sure I could give her back. I wasn't sure I wanted to.

Father Michael was expecting delivery in two days. My mother was waiting for me.

But sitting in that chair, watching Freya sleep with gauze wrapped around her feet and bruises painting her ribs, I felt the first real crack in my loyalty.

Because she was mine to fix.

And maybe; just maybe, that meant she was mine to keep.

* * * *

The truck stop was a sensory assault after the quiet confinement of the car. A cavernous space filled with the deafening clatter of cutlery, the roar of grills, and the low rumble of conversations overlaid with the static of televisions mounted in the corners. The air smelled of burnt coffee, frying bacon, and diesel fumes.

Freya shrank into the booth the moment we sat down. She pulled her hood low, hiding her face, but I could see her eyes darting nervously behind the curtain of her hair. The bandages on her feet were hidden inside her sneakers, but she moved stiffly, her bruised ribs making her wince every time she shifted.

"Eat," I said, sliding a laminated menu across the table toward her. "Protein. You need it to heal."

She nodded, keeping her head down, her finger tracing the water stains on the table surface. She looked like a bird caught in a storm, waiting for the branch to snap. Every few seconds, her eyes would dart to the door, to the windows, cataloging exits she couldn't use. Her shoulders were drawn up tight, making herself as small as possible. It was a survival instinct I recognised; the prey trying to avoid the predator's notice. But it had the opposite effect in a place like this. Weakness attracted attention.

I signalled the waitress. When she came, I ordered us both hamburgers, fries and coffee. I didn't ask Freya what she wanted. She looked too overwhelmed to make decisions, and I needed to keep this quick.

"I'll be at the register," I told her, standing up. "Don't move."

She didn't answer, just hunched further into her jacket.

I walked to the front counter to pay. The diner was packed, a mix of long-haul truckers and weary travelers. I kept my back to the room, but my senses were tuned to the booth behind me. I could hear the scrape of chairs, the chime of the door opening and closing.

Then I heard the laughter. Low and raucous, the kind of noise that usually preceded trouble.

I glanced into the reflection of a convex mirror mounted on the ceiling near the coffee station. Three men stood by our booth. Truckers, wearing flannel and grease-stained caps, looking for entertainment on a long layover. Freya was cornered. She had pressed herself as far back into the vinyl seat as she could go. One of the men leaned over the table, blocking her light.

"Hey, sweetheart," the man's reflection

showed a leer, a flash of yellow teeth. "You look a little young to be traveling alone."

Freya didn't answer. I watched her freeze. It was the same panic response she'd had on the bus; her muscles locking, her breath catching. The compound had trained her well. She didn't know how to fight back against authority or aggression. She was programmed to endure, to be invisible.

"We just want to know where your daddy is," another man chimed in, leaning closer.

I saw one of them reach out, a thick dirty hand moving toward her hood to pull it back.

My body reacted before my brain caught up. My pulse spiked, adrenaline flooding my system in a hot rush. My hands flexed at my sides, instinctively curling into fists. The cashier was saying something to me, asking about change or a receipt, but her voice was underwater, distorted and distant. All I could see was that hand reaching for Freya. All I could hear was the blood roaring in my ears.

I turned away from the counter. I didn't draw my gun. A weapon brought police, and police brought questions. I didn't need a gun to deal with trash.

I walked across the room. The crowd seemed to part around me, instinctively sensing the predator in their midst. I didn't rush. I walked with a loose, rolling gait that covered the distance in seconds. I stopped right behind the man reaching for her.

"Problem?"

My voice was low. Quiet. But it carried over the diner noise. The trucker froze, his hand hovering inches from Freya's face. He turned slowly, looking me up and down. He was big, broad-shouldered, but he was soft. The life of a trucker was sedentary. My life was violence.

"Just making conversation," the man said, puffing out his chest, though his eyes flickered with uncertainty. "She's alone."

"She's not," I said. I stepped into his space, forcing him to recoil or stand his ground. I wanted him to recoil. "She's with me."

I looked past him to Freya. She was staring up at me, her eyes wide, her chest heaving. She wasn't looking at the truckers anymore. She was looking at me. She wasn't terrified of me in that moment; she was clinging to the violence I radiated like it was a lifeline.

"Back off, buddy," the third man said from the other side of the booth, trying to sound brave. "We're just talking."

I shifted my gaze to him. I didn't blink. I let the Enforcer, the thing I had been bred to be, stare out of my eyes. I let him see the absolute lack of humanity in my expression. I took a single step toward him, closing the distance. Close enough that he could smell the threat coming off me. Close enough that he could see I wasn't bluffing. My voice dropped even lower, barely above a whisper. "You touch her, and I'll break every finger on that hand. One at a time. Understand?" I let him see that I had broken men for far less than touching what was mine.

The man swallowed hard. The bravado evaporated.

"We're leaving," the first trucker muttered, sensing the shift in the air.

They moved away, muttering among themselves, casting nervous glances back. They sat at the counter, as far from our booth as possible.

I looked down at Freya. She was trembling, a fine vibration that rattled the cutlery on the table.

"Eat," I said again. "Before I change my mind and drag you out."

I paid the cashier and waited by the door while she forced down a few bites of the burger. She didn't taste it. I could tell. She just wanted to obey so we could leave.

We walked out to the car in silence. The cool air hit us, clearing some of the grease and tension, but my blood was still boiling. We got in. I slammed my door harder than necessary. Freya sat stiffly in the passenger seat, waiting for the lecture. She curled her hands in her lap, staring at her knees.

"I..." she started, her voice small. "I didn't know what to do. I didn't want to cause a scene."

"You didn't cause a scene," I snapped, starting the engine. "You froze. Again."

"I'm sorry," she whispered.

I gripped the steering wheel until my knuckles turned white. I wanted to be angry at her. I wanted to be angry that she was weak, that she couldn't defend herself, that she was a liability. That was the Enforcer's reaction. But the Enforcer wasn't driving. The rage coursing through me wasn't the cold, calculated violence I'd been trained to wield. It was something rawer, something that clawed at my insides and demanded blood. When I'd seen that man's hand reaching for her hood, something primitive had taken over. Mine, it had snarled. Mine to protect. Mine to guard. The intensity of it scared me. I was burning with a rage so hot it felt like fever. I was furious at those men for seeing her as prey. I was furious at the world for thinking it could touch her.

"You need to be aware," I said, my voice rough. "You can't just shrink away and hope people ignore you. The world isn't the compound, Freya. People out here won't just ignore you. They'll devour you."

"I know," she said softly. "I just... I forgot. For a second, I felt like I was back there."

I looked at her. She looked small, fragile. A broken bird with taped wings.

"They thought they could touch you," I said, the words coming out low and dark. She turned to me, confused.

"What?"

"Those men. They looked at you and thought they had a right." I shifted the car into drive, peeling out of the lot and onto the highway. The trees blurred past us. "They don't," I said. "No one touches you."

"Why?" she asked. "You're taking me back to be punished. You're taking me back to... to him. Why do you care if some stranger grabs my arm?"

I didn't answer. I couldn't. Because the truth was a jagged shard of glass in my throat. I realised in that moment, with the smell of the diner still clinging to my jacket, that the dynamic had shifted. I wasn't just guarding a captive. I was protecting a woman. I didn't want the world to break her. I didn't want the universe to grind her down until she was dust. Because breaking her was my privilege. The thought hit me with the force of a physical blow. It was possessive, arrogant, and undeniably true. I was the one who had hunted her, who had hurt her, who had tied her up. I was the only one allowed to wield that kind of power over her. Anyone else who tried would have to go through me.

"You're mine," I said finally, the possessive claim hanging in the air between us. The words tasted like truth and damnation all at once. I'd crossed a line I hadn't even known existed. This wasn't about duty anymore. This wasn't about following orders or protecting the compound's property. This was something darker, something that coiled in my chest and refused to let go.

"Until I hand you over, you are mine. And I don't share."

Freya stared at me for a long moment. She didn't flinch. She didn't shrink away. She just looked at me, really looked at me, searching for the lie.

"Okay," she whispered, turning back to the window. "Okay."

She reached out, her hand drifting across the center console until her fingers rested on the fabric of my seat. Not touching me, but close. A silent acknowledgement.

I watched the road, but inside, I was watching her. The cage was getting smaller, and the predator was starting to guard the prey against the rest of the pack.

CHAPTER 19

Freya

The air in the car smelled of stale coffee and cold leather.

We were parked in a turnout overlooking a sweeping valley of pine trees. Beautiful, in a terrifying, empty way. I stared out the window, my bandaged feet throbbing with a dull, persistent heat. The world outside looked so peaceful.

Inside, I was a prisoner.

But a prisoner whose feet had been bandaged. Whose wounds had been cleaned with hands that had been surprisingly gentle. Whose ribs were wrapped with care instead of cruelty.

I didn't know what to do with that contradiction.

Andre sat in the driver's seat, his eyes on the rearview mirror, scanning the road behind us. He hadn't spoken in an hour. The silence was heavy, a physical weight that pressed against my bruised ribs.

I was acutely aware of him in the confined space. The way he breathed, slow and measured. The occasional flex of his jaw when he checked the mirror. The way his fingers drummed once, just once, against the steering wheel before going still again.

He was tense. Waiting for something. Or maybe avoiding something.

The memory of the bathroom was still too fresh. His hands on my feet. The careful way he'd pressed the antiseptic cloth to raw skin. The warmth of his shoulder when I'd leaned my forehead against it.

I'd sought comfort from my captor. And worse; he'd given it.

Then the burner phone on the dashboard chimed.

Sharp. Digital. Instantly familiar. It was the same ringtone I had heard on the phones carried by the sons. The sound of obedience.

My stomach dropped.

I turned my head slowly to look at him.

Andre didn't flinch. He picked up the phone, his expression hardening into something carved from granite. He didn't look at me as he answered.

"Andre," he said.

His voice was devoid of the rough affection he'd used at the diner. It was the voice of the soldier.

I couldn't hear the voice on the other end, but I didn't need to. I knew who it was.

Father Michael.

The air in the car seemed to thicken, to pressurise.

Andre listened for a long moment. I watched his jaw tighten, the muscle jumping beneath the stubble.

My hands curled into fists in my lap. Whatever Father Michael was saying, it wasn't good. I could tell by the way Andre's knuckles whitened on the phone, by the way his breathing changed; shallower, controlled.

This was it. This was where Andre reported everything. Where he told Father Michael I'd fought, I'd run, I'd defied every rule. Where the Enforcer stopped being gentle and became the weapon he was trained to be.

"I have her," Andre said.

His eyes flicked to me, then away.

I held my breath.

She is defiant. She fought. She tried to drown herself in the river. She is angry. Send the Breaking Squad.

Instead, he said, "She is docile."

My eyes widened. I stared at his profile, my heart hammering against my ribs.

Docile? Me? The girl who had run? Who had screamed in his face? Who threw a book at his head?

"She understands her place now," Andre continued, his voice steady.

A lie. A perfect, smooth lie.

"The flight left her."

The voice on the line spoke again. Andre's grip on the phone tightened until his knuckles turned white.

"No," he said sharply. "There is no corruption."

He looked at me then, really looked at me, his gaze locking onto mine.

I saw the ferocity there, the dark hunger that terrified and thrilled me, but beneath it, something else. A calculation. A warning. Or maybe a promise.

Don't move, his eyes seemed to say. Don't breathe. Trust me.

Trust him. The man who'd kidnapped me. The absurdity should have made me laugh.

"She is not corrupting," he said to the phone, but his eyes were boring into mine. "She is seeing the truth."

I froze.

Seeing the truth? The truth was a cage. The truth was a collar. Was he saying I had accepted that?

The voice spoke again, tinny in the silence. I imagined Father Michael's tone; warm, expectant, surgical. Then bring her to the house for immediate reintegration.

Andre hesitated.

A fraction of a second. A heartbeat.

"No," he said. "Not immediate reintegration."

I leaned forward slightly, confused.

What was he doing?

"She has been through a trauma," he said, his voice lowering, becoming persuasive. "If we break her now, she will shatter. We need her intact."

Intact.

The word settled over me like a shroud.

He listened again, then nodded, even though the caller couldn't see him.

"I will bring her to the cleansing ceremony," Andre said. "Not the breaking."

My breath hitched.

I knew the difference. Every member did.

Breaking was for the rebellious. It was the white room, the hypnosis, the erasure of self until you were a hollow shell fit only for Father Michael's will. It was a death sentence for the soul.

Cleansing was a ritual. A washing of the feet, a renewal of vows. Humiliation, yes. Submission. But it didn't destroy you. It just claimed you.

He was bargaining for my mind.

"She is ready for the ceremony," Andre said, his voice leaving no room for argument. "I will deliver her personally."

The voice on the other end spoke one last time. Andre ended the call without saying goodbye.

He tossed the phone onto the dashboard.

The silence that followed was deafening.

He stared out the windshield at the valley below. I stared at him.

My hands were trembling in my lap. I felt like I had just witnessed a murder. Or a miracle.

He'd lied. Not a small lie, not an omission. A deliberate, calculated deception to the man who controlled his entire life. The man who could destroy him with a word.

For me.

"You lied," I whispered.

"I reported our status," he corrected.

He didn't look at me.

"You told them I was docile." I laughed, a dry, incredulous sound. "Andre, I threw a book at your head. I tried to run from you. Multiple times."

"You were scared," he said, his voice rough. "And you're tired. There's no point in telling them details that will only make them angry."

"They wanted to break me," I said, the horror of it creeping up my spine. "He asked for immediate reintegration, didn't he?"

"They wanted to ensure you weren't a threat," he said.

"So you told them I was a good little bird," I said, the accusation heavy.

He turned to me then, his eyes dark and intense.

"Yes. I told them you were good. I told them you were seeing the truth."

"Why?"

He shifted in his seat, turning his body toward me. The car suddenly felt very small. His knee was inches from mine. I could smell him; the faint scent of soap from the motel, the leather of the car, something distinctly him underneath it all. Close enough that I could see the flecks of lighter colour in his dark eyes, the tiny scar on his chin I'd never noticed before.

Close enough to be dangerous in an entirely different way.

"Because if they think you're broken, Freya, they will put you in the white room. They will strap you to a chair and wipe your brain until you can't even remember your own name."

I swallowed hard.

"And you're saving me from that?"

"I'm protecting my asset," he said, but the defence sounded weak even as he said it. "I caught you. The credit for your return is mine. I won't let them ruin my work before I can present it."

I searched his face.

He was lying again. Not to Father Michael this time; to himself. To me. The excuse was too practised, too smooth. If this was about credit, about professional pride, he wouldn't have hesitated on that call. He wouldn't have risked Father Michael's anger.

This was about something else. Something he didn't want to name.

He was an enforcer. He was the one who

stood by while others were erased. But he had just spoken against the orders of the man who controlled his entire life. He had manipulated the truth to keep me whole.

He was buying me time.

"You're taking me back," I whispered, the realisation settling in. "You're still taking me to the compound."

"I have orders," he said, his jaw set.

"But you're not taking me to the breaking," I pressed. "You're taking me to a cleansing. Why does it matter to you if I'm a hollow shell or not?"

He didn't answer.

He just looked at me, his gaze tracing the bandage on my wrist, then moving up to my eyes. There was a crack in his armour, a fissure of uncertainty that I hadn't seen before.

For a heartbeat, I thought he might tell me the truth. Whatever truth he was hiding from himself. But instead he looked away, his jaw working.

"Cleansing is enough," he said finally. "It's enough."

I leaned back against the seat, my heart pounding.

He was still the enemy. Still the man with the gun, the man who carved symbols into doors. The man who'd tied my wrists and dragged me across state lines.

But he was also the man who'd bandaged my feet. Who'd pushed a sugar dispenser across a diner table. Who'd just lied to the most dangerous man either of us knew to save me from the worst fate imaginable.

I didn't know how to reconcile the violence with the tenderness. The captor with the protector.

But as he started the car and pulled back onto the highway, I realised something fundamental had shifted.

He was betraying his duty. He didn't see it as betrayal yet; he probably told himself it was about credit, about efficiency. But it was betrayal. He was choosing not to break me. He was choosing to shield me from the worst of it, even while he was still marching me toward the cage.

And in that omission, I found a terrified, strange kind of hope.

I looked out at the trees rushing by, the world blurring at the edges.

In my peripheral vision I could see his hand on the gearshift. Strong, scarred knuckles. The same hand that had cleaned my wounds. The same hand that had held a gun to my ribs.

I shouldn't want to reach out. Shouldn't want to touch him, to see if his skin was as warm as I remembered from the bathroom floor.

But I did.

And that terrified me more than anything Father Michael could do.

I was still going back.

But I wasn't going back as a broken thing to

be discarded.

I was going back as something protected.

Protected by the man who'd captured me.

Protected by the man I was starting to trust.

Protected by the man I was dangerously close to wanting.

And that was the most dangerous thought of all.

CHAPTER 20

Andre

The darkness in the motel room was absolute. I sat in the armchair by the window, watching the headlights of passing cars sweep across the ceiling like phantom searchlights. Exhausted in the way that goes past sleep; days on the road, the chase, the catch, the phone call I was still turning over in my head. But I couldn't close my eyes.

Because Freya was screaming.

It wasn't a loud noise. It was a trapped, whimpering sound that clawed its way out of her throat, raw and ragged. She thrashed against the tangled sheets, her head tossing back and forth, her limbs jerking in spasms of panic.

"Stop," she whispered. "Please. Stop."

I stood up and crossed to the bed.

I knew I should wake her. Shake her out of it. But for a moment I just stood there and listened, because what she was saying next stopped me cold.

"You will become one with us all."

The words tore out of her, distorted, twisted into something her sleeping mind was trying to fight off rather than recite. Her voice rose, high and frantic.

"You will become one with us all."

I had heard those words a thousand times. I had stood at the back of the prayer hall and watched them land. I had watched girls fold under the weight of them, watched the chant strip something essential away until what was left knelt quietly and called it peace.

I had said them myself. Twice, at induction ceremonies. The words had tasted like nothing in my mouth. Efficient. Necessary. True.

They didn't taste like nothing now.

I reached out and grabbed her shoulders, shaking her firmly.

"Freya. Wake up."

Her eyes flew open. Wide, unfocused, filled with a terror so total it hit me like a fist. She didn't see me. She saw the locked house. She saw the white room.

"No!"

She lunged upward, swinging wildly. I caught her wrists, pinning them to the mattress, using my weight to hold her down.

"Freya. It's me. It's Andre."

She froze beneath me, her chest heaving.

Recognition swam in slowly through the terror. When it arrived, it didn't bring relief. Her expression cycled through shame, confusion, and something else underneath that I didn't let myself name.

"Andre," she breathed. Her voice was wrecked.

"You were dreaming about the house," I said, keeping my voice low. "About the words."

She turned her face away, pressing her cheek hard into the pillow.

"Don't. Don't talk about it."

"I've heard those words a thousand times," I said. The confession came out before I could stop it, heavy and wrong-tasting. "I've said them. I've watched them break people."

She looked back at me then, her eyes cutting through the dark.

"And do you still believe them? Do you still think it's peace, Andre? Or do you know it's just a cage?"

I looked down at her. My mother's face was somewhere behind that question, her fingers smoothing the silver compass against her chest, her eyes soft with a contentment I had spent my whole life protecting. I had built my purpose on the answer being yes. On the peace being real.

"I don't know," I admitted.

The honesty stripped me raw. The air between us changed.

I was still holding her wrists. She had

stopped trying to pull away. Her breathing was evening out, the nightmare receding, but she wasn't retreating from me the way she usually did. She was looking up at me with those exhausted, furious, searching eyes, and something in her expression was asking a question she hadn't put into words yet.

"Then prove it," she whispered. "Stop looking at me like I'm a victim."

My control didn't snap loudly. It went quietly, the way a rope frays; one thread at a time until it simply gives.

I wasn't rough the way I had been before. This wasn't the Enforcer taking what the mission permitted. I released her wrists and my hand moved to her jaw instead, tilting her face up, making her look at me.

"Careful what you ask for, little bird."

She didn't look away. That was what undid me. Every other time, there had been fear underneath everything, and I had told myself that was the correct order of things. But she was looking at me now with her eyes open and her jaw set and something that wasn't fear at all, and I couldn't find a word for what I was supposed to do with that.

My thumb traced the line of her jaw. She exhaled slowly, the last of the nightmare leaving her body in that single breath.

I could see the memories clawing at the edges of her mind; in the frantic twitch at her eye, the way her breath hitched. Flashes of screams in the dark, hands that weren't mine but had felt just as inescapable. The kind of trauma that burrowed deep and festered. She'd run from that life only to crash into this one, where escape was a joke and pleasure twisted into chains.

My fingers traced the faint red line on her inner thigh from the knife I had used last time, light as a breath. Not the sharp bite from before; just a whisper of pressure against already-sensitised skin.

"This isn't just about control," I said. My thumb circled the spot slowly, sending a shiver up her spine; part ache, part unwelcome spark. "I see it in you, little bird. The way you fight, the way you break. It's like looking in a mirror sometimes." My face was close, jaw tight, eyes shadowed with a flicker of doubt I hadn't meant to show.

"What do you know about it?" she spat, but there was no fire left; just a weary rasp. Even as she pushed me away with words, her body betrayed her, leaning into my hand despite itself. She was starving for touch that didn't destroy her, even if she couldn't admit it.

"More than you think," I replied, my free hand sliding up her arm.

My fingers grazed the curve of her breast; not grabbing, not demanding, just a slow deliberate stroke that made her nipple pebble under her shirt. I watched her body arch instinctively toward me, that helpless lean she hated herself for. I coaxed her thighs to part slightly, a subtle pressure that bordered on discomfort before I soothed it with the warmth of my palm cupping her breast fully.

"Tell me," I urged, my lips brushing her temple, my voice a low rumble that I knew vibrated through her. "What haunts you in the dark? The same things that keep me up, wondering if I'm the villain or just a fool chasing ghosts?"

My words cracked something open in her. A sob escaped; raw and unfiltered. She clutched at my shirt, her nails digging in just enough to leave half-moons in my skin, a tiny retaliation that made me hiss softly. The sound stirred a dark satisfaction in me; she marked me as I marked her. I didn't pull away. Instead I tilted her chin up, my mouth claiming hers in a kiss that started soft, exploratory; nothing like what had come before.

I tasted the salt on her lips. My tongue teased them apart and when she yielded it delved deeper, tasting tears and heat. Pleasure unfurled slowly between us.

My hand drifted lower, fingers splaying over her stomach before sliding between her legs. She was already wet, slick and hot against my fingertips. I didn't thrust. I petted, stroking her with featherlight touches that pulled gasps into my mouth. I wanted to learn her; to map the topography of her want rather than her fear. A slight press against her clit sent a mild sting through the oversensitive nub, more tease than torment, quickly chased by slow circles that built a sweet throbbing ache.

"I push you because I know you can take it," I breathed against her lips, nipping her lower one just hard enough to tingle, not bruise. "But maybe I'm pushing myself too. Questioning if this, us, is salvation or just another cage."

She moaned, the sound vibrating against my mouth, her hips rocking greedily into my hand. The confession wove through the haze of sensation. She was letting go.

My fingers slipped inside her, shallow and unhurried, curling to find that inner spot while my thumb continued its lazy rhythm on her clit. The faint stretch pulled at sore muscles; a whisper of discomfort that heightened the pleasure, making each slow glide feel like velvet over embers. She was so tight, so hot around me, her walls gripping each deliberate curl of my fingers. I added a second, feeling her gasp against my mouth, her back arching off the mattress as I worked her open slowly, unhurrying, learning every sound she made and filing each one away.

Her free hand wandered to my belt, fumbling with the buckle. I stiffened. She wasn't doing it to fight; she was reaching for me, trying to touch me, to ground herself in the heat of my body. I groaned low in my throat as she freed me, hard and heavy in her palm. The sensation of her hand; tentative at first, then growing bolder, her fingers wrapping around me and stroking with a curiosity that was going to undo me entirely; nearly shattered my resolve. I rocked into her grip once, just once, before I caught myself.

I captured her wrist, bringing her hand to my chest instead, letting her feel the rapid hammering beat under her palm.

"Not tonight," I said, my voice rough with the effort of it. "This is about you, not me."

I left her hand over my heart and wrapped my other hand around her throat; not the belt's vice, but a firm hold that restricted just enough to spark that familiar euphoria in her eyes. A light-headed float, colours softening at the edges, every touch amplified. The pressure built gradually, her breaths coming shorter and shallower, the tightening at her throat making every stroke of my fingers inside her feel twice as deep. I watched her face, the way her mind loosened like silk threads unravelling, pleasure swelling in warm waves that lapped at the ache in her neck.

I wanted to ruin her. I found, terrifyingly, that I also wanted to save her. The duality sat in my chest like a live wire.

She came undone slowly. A soft cresting that left her shuddering against me, her walls fluttering around my fingers in gentle pulses, her thighs clamping tight as the orgasm moved through her in long rolling waves. A release that washed the trauma's sharp edges back for a stolen moment, replacing them with the heat of my skin. I held her through it, loosening my grip on her throat to let the air flood back. The rush of oxygen intensified the afterglow into something languid and blurred, her whole body going loose against mine.

No more pushing. No more questions. Just my arms around her and the darkness a fraction less absolute.

She lay limp against me, skin flushed, eyes wet. Her breathing slowed and I rolled onto my back and stared at the ceiling.

I was bred to break her. I had just held her together.

The guilt sat cold in my gut; not the clean guilt of an enforcer who had overstepped, but something with no name in Father Michael's vocabulary. I was the one who kept the monster fed. But lying there in the dark, listening to her breathe, I knew I had crossed a line I couldn't find my way back from.

I no longer wanted to deliver her to the Leader.

Step by reluctant step, I was beginning to question everything I had ever called purpose.

CHAPTER 21

Freya

The next morning, the silence in the car was different. It wasn't just tense; it was heavy with the things we hadn't said. I sat in the passenger seat, my knees pulled up to my chest, watching the trees blur past. My body felt different, sore, used, but strangely awake. The shame was still there, a lingering echo in the back of my mind, but it was quieter now. Buried under the memory of how it felt to stop thinking. To stop fighting the current and just drown in it.

Andre didn't look at me. He drove with a white-knuckled grip on the wheel, his jaw set in a hard line. But I saw the way his eyes kept flicking to the rearview mirror, checking not for cops, but for something else.

I wondered if he was checking for himself. For the version of him that knew what he was supposed to do versus the version that had held me through the night instead of just using me and rolling away.

The radio was off. The only sounds were the hum of the engine and the occasional crunch of gravel when he veered too close to the shoulder. I watched his profile, the sharp line of his jaw, the tension in his shoulders. He looked like a man at war with himself.

"You're stalling," I said softly.

It wasn't an accusation, just an observation. He didn't answer immediately.

"We have plenty of time."

"We don't," I said. "Every mile we drive, I feel the walls closing in. You feel it too. I know you do."

His knuckles went whiter on the wheel. A muscle jumped in his jaw.

"You don't know anything about what I feel."

"I know you didn't sleep last night," I said. "I heard you get up three times. I heard you standing by the window, just... breathing. Like you were trying to remember how."

He sighed, a harsh exhale of breath.

"You talk too much."

"I'm not the only one thinking it," I pressed. "Last night... the way you looked at me. Andre, you hesitated. You've never hesitated before."

The words landed like stones in water, sending ripples through the silence. His jaw clenched so hard I heard his teeth grind.

He slammed on the brakes. The car veered

onto the gravel shoulder, dust billowing around us. He turned to me, his eyes fierce, wilder than I'd ever seen them.

"I am an enforcer, Freya," he growled. "I do not hesitate. I bring defectors back. I ensure order."

"Then do it," I challenged him, my heart hammering against my ribs. "Take me to the gates. Deliver me to Father Michael."

The name tasted like ash in my mouth, but I needed to push him. I needed to know which version of him was going to win.

He stared at me, his chest heaving. For a long, agonizing moment, the silence stretched between us, a tightrope strung over an abyss of shared damage.

I could see the war happening behind his eyes. The enforcer who had been trained to follow orders without question versus the man who had confessed his doubts in the dark. The weapon versus the person wielding it.

Then he cursed, a low, vile word, and slammed his hand against the steering wheel.

"Get out," he ordered.

"What?"

"Get out. Now."

He opened his door and stormed out into the woods lining the highway. I scrambled after him, confused, my heart racing. The sun was high, filtering through the pines, the air crisp with autumn chill.

"What are we doing?" I asked, following him deeper into the tree line.

He didn't answer until we were far enough from the road that the sound of passing cars was just a distant whisper. The forest swallowed us, pine needles soft under my feet, the smell of earth and sap thick in my nose.

He stopped in a small clearing and turned to face me. He rolled up his sleeves, revealing the corded muscle of his forearms. There were scars there I hadn't noticed before; thin white lines that looked like they'd been made deliberately, precisely.

"You want to survive? You want to stop being a victim? Then you need to learn how to fight."

"I already tried to fight you," I shot back. "It didn't work."

"You clawed. You bit. You ran," he said, correcting me with a dark precision. "That's not fighting. That's panic."

He was right, and I hated that he was right. Every time I'd tried to escape, every time I'd tried to resist, it had been pure animal instinct. No strategy. No control. Just terror.

"Then teach me," I said, squaring my shoulders. "Teach me how to fight like you."

Something flickered in his eyes; approval, maybe, or surprise. He nodded once.

"First lesson: never telegraph your moves. Your eyes give you away. You look where you're about to strike."

"I don't—"

He moved faster than I could track. He lunged, sweeping my legs out from under me. I hit the ground hard, the breath knocking out of me.

"Get up," he commanded.

I scrambled to my feet, wiping dirt from my jeans.

"You're enjoying this."

"I'm trying to keep you alive," he snapped.

But there was something else in his voice. Not enjoyment, exactly. Purpose. Like this was the only thing that made sense to him right now; reducing everything to bodies in motion, to the simple physics of attack and defence.

For the next two hours, he drilled me. He taught me how to break a grip, how to use an attacker's weight against them, how to strike. He was rough, relentless, a teacher who didn't tolerate excuses.

"Eyes are soft," he said, demonstrating a thumb strike in slow motion. "Throat is vulnerable. Solar plexus if you can get the angle. Never go for places that are hard; skull, chest, shoulders. You'll hurt yourself more than them."

Every time I fell, he demanded I get up. Every time I hesitated, he shouted until I moved.

"Faster! You think an attacker is going to wait while you think about it?"

"I'm trying!"

"Trying gets you killed."

He grabbed me from behind, his arm around my throat in a chokehold. Panic surged, the old fear flooding back.

"What do you do?" he demanded in my ear.

I froze, my hands scrabbling uselessly at his forearm.

"Freya. What. Do. You. Do?"

"I—I don't—"

"Tuck your chin. Protect your airway. Then drop your weight and twist toward my elbow, not away from it. Break my structure."

He loosened his grip just enough for me to breathe. I tried to remember, tried to make my body do what he'd taught me. Chin down. Drop. Twist toward the elbow—

I broke free, stumbling forward and whirling to face him.

"Better," he said. "Again."

We did it again. And again. And again until the panic started to fade, until my body began to remember what my mind forgot in the moment of fear.

But somewhere between the sweat and the bruises, the dynamic shifted. It wasn't just captor and captive anymore. He was showing me how to inhabit the body I had never been taught to use. He was treating me like a weapon, not a doll.

And I found myself responding. Not with fear, but with fierce, burning determination. Every fall became a lesson. Every bruise became a reminder that I could take the hit and get back up. He was teaching me not just how to fight, but how to be dangerous.

"You're getting sloppy," he said after I'd managed to slip one of his grabs. "Your footwork is all wrong."

"Then fix it."

He stepped behind me, his hands on my hips, adjusting my stance. The touch was impersonal, clinical, but I felt the heat of him anyway.

"Feet shoulder-width apart. Knees soft, not locked. You want to be able to move in any direction without thinking about it."

His hands slid down to my thighs, tapping the inside of my knee.

"Here. This is your power centre. Every strike, every movement, starts here."

I was acutely aware of how close he was standing, how his breath stirred my hair. But he wasn't doing this to seduce me. He was doing this because he actually cared whether I could defend myself.

When he pinned me for the tenth time, his hand wrapped around my throat, forcing me into the dirt, I didn't panic. I looked him in the eye. I felt the pulse of his wrist against my skin, the heat of his body leaning into mine.

"Is this how you train everyone?" I asked, my voice husky.

"No," he said, his gaze dropping to my lips. "Just you."

He didn't let me go. He held me there, his thumb pressing against my jugular, just enough pressure to make me dizzy. I didn't want to run. I wanted him to close the distance.

The realisation should have terrified me. This was the man who'd hunted me, who'd dragged me back, who'd held a belt around my throat while I came apart. But somehow, in this clearing with dirt under my nails and sweat on my skin, I wanted him to kiss me more than I'd wanted anything.

"Andre," I whispered.

I didn't know what I was asking for. I just knew I wanted more.

He groaned, a sound of frustration and hunger, and crushed his mouth to mine.

This wasn't like the night before. This wasn't roughness or punishment. This was a collision. I arched up into him, my hands tangling in his hair, pulling him closer. I wanted him to consume me. I wanted the violence to turn into something else.

His tongue swept into my mouth, tasting of coffee and desperation. One hand stayed at my throat, not squeezing, just holding, while the other braced beside my head. That restraint; the care in it even now, made something crack open in my chest.

I pulled back just enough to breathe, my lips already swollen.

"Don't stop," I said. "Please don't stop."

He pulled back, his breathing ragged, his eyes dark.

"I can't. Not here. Not like this."

"Why not?" I asked, reaching for him. "I want this. I want you."

The confession hung in the air, shocking and true. I was asking for the touch that once would have been forced on me. I was reclaiming this, reclaiming him.

He looked at me for a long moment, seeing the honesty in my eyes. Something shifted in his expression; understanding, maybe, or recognition.

"You don't know what you're asking," he said quietly.

"Yes, I do. I'm asking you to want me. Not as a captive. Not as a mission. As me."

His hand tightened fractionally on my throat, then released. He sat back on his heels, running both hands through his hair.

"Freya—"

"I'm not confused," I interrupted. "I'm not broken or delusional. I know exactly what this is. You're the first person who's ever treated me like I could be more than a victim. The first person who's looked at me and seen something worth teaching instead of just something to use."

He stared at me, his expression unreadable.

"That's a low bar."

"It's my bar," I said. "And you cleared it."

Then he cursed again, softer this time, and

pulled me to my feet.

"Not yet," he said, his voice thick with restraint. "When I take you, Freya, it won't be in the dirt. And it won't be because you're trying to prove something. It'll be because you're mine."

The possessiveness in his voice should have frightened me. Instead it sent a shiver down my spine that had nothing to do with fear.

"Yours," I repeated, testing the weight of it.

"Little bird," he murmured, brushing a stray hair away from my face with a tenderness that made my chest ache. "You have no idea what you're agreeing to."

I thought I did. I thought he meant his control, his dominance. I didn't realise yet that he was talking about his soul.

He helped me brush the dirt and pine needles off my clothes, his touches still careful, still restrained. The training session was over, but something else had begun.

"We should get back to the car," he said finally.

"And then what?"

He looked at me, and for the first time since I'd met him, I saw uncertainty in his eyes.

"I don't know," he admitted. "I don't know anymore."

It was the most honest thing he'd ever said to me.

CHAPTER 22

Andre

The only sound was the ragged rhythm of our breathing and the rustle of pine needles settling around us. The training session had ended minutes ago, but the adrenaline still hummed in my blood.

Freya stood opposite me, rubbing her bruised forearm, her face flushed with the exertion. She looked alive. More alive than she had been in the compound, more alive than she had ever been. Violence suited her. It gave her a focus other than fear.

I leaned against the trunk of a tree, wiping sweat from my forehead with the back of my hand. The air was cool, a stark contrast to the heat of the sparring. My knuckles ached from where she'd actually managed to block one of my strikes; not perfectly, but enough to show she was learning. Fast.

Too fast for someone I was supposed to be delivering back into captivity.

"Why bother?"

I looked over at her. She was watching me, her brows drawn together.

"Teaching me to fight," she clarified, nodding at the clearing where we'd just spent the last hour. "If I'm just going back there. If I'm just going to be a good little bird and kneel at the Leader's feet... why teach me how to break a nose or throw a punch?"

I clenched my fists. It was a valid question. Illogical. I was creating a weapon out of a runaway, a risk to the very order I was sworn to protect.

The question exposed the contradiction I'd been trying not to examine. Every enforcer knew the rules: retrieve the asset, return them broken enough to obey but whole enough to serve. Don't improve them. Don't strengthen them. Don't give them the tools to be dangerous.

And here I was, teaching her leverage points and strike zones like she was a recruit instead of a prisoner.

"Because I have to," I said, the words coming out rougher than I intended.

Even as I said it, I knew it was weak. A deflection. The truth was more complicated and far more damning.

The truth was that somewhere between the river and the motel rooms, between the belt around her throat and the way she'd looked at me with something other than fear, I'd started to care whether she lived or died. Not just as cargo to be delivered. As a person.

That realisation terrified me more than any fight I'd ever been in.

"That's not an answer," she countered, her voice tired but edged with defiance. "You want obedience. You broke me for running. Why give me the tools to do it again?"

I pushed off the tree and walked over to her, standing close enough that she had to tilt her head back to look at me.

"Because the journey back isn't safe," I said. "And because if you go back weak, if you go back broken, they will destroy you. The Leader doesn't want a victim anymore, Freya. He wants an example. He wants someone who has seen the world and chosen us anyway. If I deliver you trembling and afraid, you're useless to him."

It was a half-truth. A justification I crafted on the spot. But it wasn't the whole truth.

The real truth was that I couldn't stand the idea of her being helpless. Couldn't stand the thought of delivering her back only for her to be at the mercy of every man who decided she was fair game. At least if she knew how to fight, she'd have a chance.

A chance at what, though? Survival in a cage was still a cage.

She searched my eyes, looking for the lie.

"So you're toughening me up for the slaughter."

The words hit harder than they should have. Because she was right. That was exactly what I was doing; making her strong enough to endure what was coming. Like fattening a lamb before the sacrifice.

"I'm making sure you survive the trip," I corrected.

She looked away, staring at the dark line of the trees.

"And why does it matter to you? Why do you stay? Why do you enforce these rules?"

The question hung there, heavier than the silence. No one had ever asked me why. I was an enforcer. I was the wall. I simply was. But looking at her; this girl who had run through a river to escape the life I protected, I felt the need to explain. I wanted her to understand the architecture of my cage.

"Because I owe them everything," I said, the confession scraping my throat.

I sat down on the cold ground, Freya following suit, leaving a foot of space between us. I needed to not look at her when I said this.

"My mother," I started. "Before the compound... she was nothing. We were nothing."

I saw the image of her in my mind; not the serene woman who wore the necklace now, but the hollowed-out ghost I remembered from my childhood. The woman who shook in the corner of dirty apartments while men with belts and bottles walked through the door.

"We lived in squalor," I said, the word bitter on my tongue. "Real squalor, Freya. Not the freedom you ran to. Rot and filth. Hunger that makes you eat things that aren't food. Men who treat you like a tissue to be used and tossed."

I remembered stealing food from gas stations when I was seven. The taste of spoiled milk because it was the only thing in the fridge. My mother's hollow eyes when she came home from whatever job or john she'd been with, smelling like smoke and shame.

I remembered the night a man had broken her arm. She told me it was an accident, that she fell. I was five and I believed her because believing was easier than knowing the truth. The Leader set that arm. He held her while she cried. He gave her pills for the pain and told her she was safe now.

And she had been. The men stopped coming. The fear stopped. The hunger stopped.

But something else had stopped too. Something I couldn't name until I saw it burning in Freya's eyes.

Freya shifted, turning her body toward me. She was listening. She wasn't judging.

"The cult found us," I continued. "Father Michael found us. He gave us a roof. He gave us food. He gave her a purpose. He told her she wasn't trash. He told her she was a daughter of the light."

I remembered the way she had looked at the Leader, tears of gratitude streaming down her face. The way she had knelt at his feet and kissed his ring. It was the first time I had ever seen her smile.

"He saved her," I said. "He took a woman who was dying from the inside out and gave her a life worth living. I enforce the rules to keep that world safe for her. I do it to repay a debt I can never balance."

I looked at Freya then, expecting her to see the logic. To see the nobility in sacrifice.

But as I spoke the words aloud, they sounded hollow. They sounded like ash in my mouth.

I looked at Freya; the girl who had run into the squalor to save her soul. She had slept in motels with peeling paint. She had eaten from gas station dumpsters. She had walked until her feet bled. And she had done it all with a fire in her eyes that my mother hadn't had in twenty years.

My mother was safe. She was fed. She was clothed.

But she was also hollow. She wore a necklace that marked her as property. She smiled at a man who turned her sons into weapons. She spoke in rehearsed phrases about light and purpose and unity. When was the last time I'd heard her laugh? When was the last time she'd had a thought that wasn't scripted by the Leader's sermons?

Freya was bruised. She was hunted. She was

terrified.

But she was whole.

The logic shattered.

I was on my feet before I knew I'd moved.

My fist hit the tree trunk so hard the bark split under my knuckles. I didn't stop. I hit it again, the rough wood shredding skin, the impact cracking up through my wrist and elbow and shoulder, and I welcomed every bit of it because it was real, because it was the only real thing left. Blood welled across my knuckles, dark in the low light, and I stared at it for half a second before the air came out of me in something that wasn't a breath, wasn't a word, wasn't anything I could name.

My back hit the trunk. I slid down it.

Pine needles pressed into my palms. The cold of the ground soaked through my jeans. I was staring at nothing, at the dark shapes of the trees, at the thin strip of grey sky between the branches, and the thoughts were coming too fast and too loud, the kind that don't arrive in sentences, just in images. My mother's hollow eyes over a kitchen table that always smelled of damp. The creak of a floorboard that meant don't move, don't breathe, don't exist. Her arm in a sling, her smile when she said she fell, the careful way she never looked at me when she said it. Father Michael's hand on her shoulder and the way she leaned into it like a flower turning toward light. The sound of her laugh the day we arrived at the compound, the first time I had ever heard it.

I had given everything to protect that laugh.

Twenty years. Twenty years of being the wall, the hand that corrects, the shadow that frightens. Twenty years of believing it was love by another name. That obedience was the only currency that meant anything, the only way to keep the one person in the world who had needed me breathing and upright and whole.

And the whole time I had been feeding her to the same machine I served.

My hand was bleeding steadily now, a slow drip onto the pine needles, and I watched it like it was happening to someone else. My chest felt wrong, too tight and too hollow at once, like something structural had given way inside and the walls hadn't caught up yet. I couldn't get ahead of it. Every time I tried to find solid ground there was just more of it, more of the lie, layer under layer under layer, and underneath all of it was a boy who was six years old eating spoiled food in the dark and calling it salvation because someone had told him it was.

I didn't hear her move.

But I felt her.

Her hand came to rest between my shoulder blades, low and steady, her palm flat against my back. She didn't crouch beside me or try to see my face. She just stood there, her hand a warm point of pressure through my shirt, and stayed.

She didn't speak.

She didn't try to name it or fix it or pull me back from it. She just kept her hand there and let the silence be what it was, and something about that; about being witnessed without being managed, broke something open in my chest that was different from the rage. Quieter. Worse.

I had held her through nightmares. Through pain I had caused. Through the aftermath of everything I had done to her, and she was standing here with her palm on my back like she had known how to do this all along.

Like she had been waiting for her turn.

I don't know how long we stayed like that. Long enough for my breathing to find a rhythm again. Long enough for the worst of it to move through me and leave something still in its place.

I straightened slowly. My hand was throbbing. The bark had taken most of the skin from two knuckles.

I didn't turn around yet.

I looked at my hands; the hands that had just taught her how to strike, how to gouge, how to survive. Why had I done that? To make her a better offering for the Leader?

No.

I had done it because I wanted her to live.

The realisation hit me like a physical blow. The debt to my mother didn't cover this. It didn't cover destroying this girl just to keep the peace.

My mother had made her choice when she knelt at the Leader's feet all those years ago. She'd chosen safety over freedom. Comfort over truth. And maybe that was the right choice for her; maybe she really did need the structure, the certainty, the sense of purpose the compound gave her.

But Freya had made a different choice. She'd chosen truth over comfort. Freedom over safety. And I was the one trying to drag her back into the cage she'd fought so hard to escape.

What kind of man did that make me?

Not the kind my mother thought she'd raised. Not the loyal soldier the Leader had trained. Someone in between. Someone broken in a different way.

I thought about what would happen if I went through with it. If I drove Freya back to the compound, handed her over to the Leader, watched him lead her into that locked house where girls went to have their spirits carefully dismantled. I'd get praised. Rewarded. My mother would look at me with pride. The Leader would call me his most faithful servant.

And every night for the rest of my life, I'd see Freya's face. The way she'd looked at me in the motel room when I'd chosen to hold her instead of hurt her. The way she'd stood in this clearing, bruised and sweating, learning to fight because some part of her still believed she could survive.

I'd see her, and I'd know I'd killed her. Not with my hands, but with my obedience.

"Andre?" Freya's voice was soft. She reached

out, her hand hovering over mine. "You look like you're in pain."

I turned my hand over, palm up. I didn't pull away.

"The logic... it's broken," I whispered, more to myself than to her. "The story... it doesn't work anymore."

"What do you mean?"

I looked up, meeting her gaze.

The fear was still there, but the defiance was stronger. She wasn't looking at me like the Enforcer anymore. She was looking at the man holding the leash. And I knew, with a terrifying certainty, that I could no longer be that man.

"I can't take you back there," I said, the words barely audible.

She froze. Her eyes widened.

"What?"

"I said... I can't take you back." The conviction settled over me, heavy and irreversible. "If I take you through those gates, Freya, I'm killing you. And I can't do that to my mother's son. I can't do it to you."

"But... the debt," she stammered. "Your mother."

"My mother made her choice," I said, the truth cutting deep. "And now, I have to make mine."

I stood up, the decision settling into my bones. The Leader expected a soldier. He expected a weapon. He expected me to drag his property home.

Instead, I was going to war.

I offered her my hand. She stared at it, then up at my face. She saw the shift. She saw the line I had crossed in the dirt.

Then she took my hand and held on.

CHAPTER 23

Andre

We didn't get back in the car for a long time. We sat on a fallen log near the clearing, the silence between us settling into something that felt almost like peace. But my phone buzzed in my pocket, shattering the moment. It was the Leader. I stood up, walking a few feet away to answer it. I felt Freya's eyes on my back, a weight I was becoming increasingly aware of.

"Andre," the Leader's voice was smooth, like oil over water. "You have been delayed."

"There were... complications," I said, my voice steady.

I was lying. It was the second time I had ever lied to him, and the taste of it was bitter.

"Find her," the Leader said, already assuming she had escaped me after we last spoke. "The girl is important. She carries the potential for great unity. Do not disappoint me."

"I understand," I said. "I am close."

"You have seven days," he said. "Then I will send others."

The line went dead. I stood there for a long time, the phone burning a hole in my hand. Unity. I knew what that meant now. I had seen the girls come out of the locked house. I had seen Freya's nightmares. The Leader didn't want to save her. He wanted to hollow her out.

I looked back at Freya. She was sitting on the log, her arms wrapped around her knees, watching the leaves fall. She looked small, fragile. But I knew better now. I had seen her fight. I had seen her fire.

I walked back to her.

"What did he say?" she asked.

"That we have seven days," I said.

She nodded, looking down at her hands.

"So what do we do? Where do we go?" she asked, looking up, her eyes searching mine.

"Somewhere safe," I said. "Somewhere we can figure out what to do."

"And what do we do about your mother?" she asked softly, hitting the exact nerve I knew she would.

I closed my eyes, the image of my mother's smiling face flashing in my mind. She knelt in devotion every day. She believed the Leader was a god. If I defied him, if I ran, I wasn't just damning myself. I was damning her.

"I don't know," I said, the truth scraping my throat. "But I can't take you back there, Freya. I can't let him turn you into them."

She reached out, her hand covering mine. Her fingers were cold, her grip tight.

"Then we fight. Together."

I looked at her. She wasn't the little bird anymore. She was something else. Something forged in the fire of our clash.

"Maybe together we can burn it down."

The resolve in her voice terrified me. It also made me want her more than I had ever wanted anything. Her hunger for sensation, her desire to fight, to destroy the thing that had made me; it was the most beautiful thing I had ever seen.

"We need a plan," I said, squeezing her hand. "We need to be smart."

"I know," she said. She stood up, pulling me with her. She looked at me, her eyes dark with a mix of fear and desire. "But first, Andre. You promised me. Not in the dirt. And not because I'm proving something."

I looked around. The car was visible through the trees, but here, in this clearing, we were hidden. Alone. I stepped closer, backing her up against the rough bark of a pine tree. I used my body to block the wind, the world, everything but her.

"Are you sure?" I asked, my voice dropping to a growl. "Once I start, Freya, I won't stop. I can't."

"I'm sure," she whispered. "I want this. I want

you."

Our lips met in a searing kiss. Not a question, but a statement. Her mouth was warm, yielding, and tasted of forest air. My tongue slid against hers, a deliberate invasion, and she met it with equal fervor, her teeth catching my lower lip in a sharp, perfect bite that sent a jolt straight through me.

I pulled back just enough to growl, "Mine."

Freya's eyes, dark as the soil beneath us, glittered with defiance and pure, unadulterated heat.

"Prove it."

My hands were already on her, roving over the worn cotton of her dress, mapping the landscape of her through the fabric. I found the curve of her hip, the dip of her waist, the shocking heat of the small of her back where her dress had ridden up. I worshipped her with my touch, my lips finding the pulse point on her neck, sucking until she gasped and her head lolled back against the rough bark of the pine.

This was different. Not the frantic collision from before. This was a slow, deliberate unravelling. I wanted to taste every inch of her. I dropped to my knees in the moss. My hands slid up her bare thighs, pushing the simple skirt up past her knees, her trembling thighs. The cool night air kissed her skin and she shivered. I pressed my face against the thin cotton of her panties, and the scent of her arousal; musky, sweet, profoundly her, hit me like a physical blow.

"Fuck," I breathed, the word a cloud of steam against the damp fabric. I hooked my fingers into the waistband. "Look at me."

Her gaze dropped, heavy-lidded and dark. I held it as I pulled the panties down her legs, letting them fall to the forest floor. Exposed her completely to me and the moonlight. She was bare, glistening, beautifully swollen. My mouth watered. I didn't speak again. I leaned in. My tongue, flat and broad, licked a slow, torturous path from her entrance all the way up to the tight, hard bud of her clit. She cried out, a sharp, broken sound. Her hands fisted in my hair, not pushing me away, but holding me there.

"Andre..."

I learned her. With my mouth, my tongue, my lips. I traced circles around her clit, then sucked it gently between my lips, flicking it with the tip of my tongue. Her thighs trembled against my ears. Her taste exploded on my tongue; salt, honey, and something wild, something untamed. I slid one finger inside her, then another. She was so wet, so impossibly tight and hot. I curled my fingers, searching, and found the spot that made her entire body jolt.

"There!" she gasped, her hips bucking forward, fucking herself on my hand. "Right there, don't stop, please don't stop."

I didn't. I sucked her clit into my mouth, applying steady, rhythmic pressure while my fingers worked inside her, curling and stroking that perfect, rough patch. I could feel her body coiling, tightening around my fingers, a spring wound to its breaking point. Her moans were a continuous, desperate melody in the silent woods.

"Andre, please," she begged, her voice ragged. Her nails scraped my scalp. "I need you. I need you inside me. Now."

I ignored her pleas, determined to drag out her pleasure as long as I could. I moved my fingers faster and sucked at her clit harder until she came undone, her orgasm soaking my lips and fingers. I stood so fast the world tilted. My clothes were a blur, shed in frantic, graceless movements. My cock sprang free, hard and aching, the tip already wet with my own need. I lifted her effortlessly, her legs locking around my waist, her back against the rough tree trunk. I positioned myself at her entrance, the head of my cock nudging through her slick folds. I locked my eyes on hers.

"Last chance," I growled, my voice thick, barely human. "Tell me to stop."

A wicked, triumphant smile touched her kiss-swollen lips. Her eyes held no fear, only hunger.

"Fuck me, Andre."

I slammed into her. One smooth, deep, complete stroke, burying myself to the hilt in her incredible, clutching heat. Her scream wasn't of pain, but of pure, shocked fulfilment. Her head slammed back against the tree, her eyes squeezing shut. I stayed there, embedded, letting us both feel the full, overwhelming reality of the connection. I could feel her inner muscles fluttering around me, adjusting, gripping.

"Look at me," I commanded, my breath coming in harsh pants.

Her eyes fluttered open, glazed with pleasure. I began to move. Slow at first. Withdrawing almost completely, then sliding back in with a deep, rolling thrust that made her whimper. I set a punishing rhythm, my hips driving into her, the sound of our bodies meeting; skin on skin, the rustle of bark, filling the clearing. Her breasts, freed from her dress, bounced with each impact. I leaned in and captured one taut nipple in my mouth, sucking hard.

"Harder," she panted, her heels digging into the small of my back. "God, yes, just like that."

I obeyed. My thrusts became harder, faster, driving her body up the tree with their force. The world narrowed to this: the slap of flesh, her choked cries, the exquisite friction of her clenching around me. I could feel my own orgasm building, a tidal wave in my gut. But I wanted hers first. I shifted my angle slightly, and on the next deep plunge, she shattered.

"Andre!" Her scream was raw, ripped from her throat.

Her body convulsed around me, a series of

violent, exquisite clenches that tore a groan from my own chest. Her inner walls fluttered and pulsed, drenching me in a fresh wave of her heat. The sensation was too much. My control snapped. With a final, brutal thrust, I buried myself as deep as I could go and came. My vision whited out. My whole body shook with the force of it, my hips stuttering against hers as I emptied every drop.

For a long moment, the only sounds were our ragged, mingled breaths and the distant call of an owl. Our foreheads rested together. I was still inside her, still throbbing, still intimately connected. Her legs slowly loosened their grip around my waist, but she didn't let go. And in the aftermath, as we leaned against the tree with leaves tangled in her hair, I knew I was never letting her go.

I was going to war for her.

CHAPTER 24

Andre

The car needed gas. It was a mundane necessity, a mechanical pause in a journey that felt increasingly surreal. The tank was nearing empty, the needle hovering over the red line, and the silence in the cab was getting heavy.

I'd been driving for hours, putting distance between us and the clearing, though I wasn't entirely sure where we were going. Just away. Always away. The highway stretched ahead like a promise we couldn't quite believe in.

I pulled off the highway, the transition from the rumble of asphalt to the crunch of gravel jarring. The sun was dipping low, casting long golden shadows across the parking lot. It looked peaceful. It looked like any other Tuesday in America.

Ordinary people doing ordinary things. Filling up their tanks. Buying lottery tickets. Checking their phones. Living lives that didn't involve running from cults or planning murders.

I envied them.

"Get us something to eat and pay for the gas," I said to Freya, putting the car in park. "I'll pump."

She nodded, climbing out of the car and heading inside. I watched her go, noting the way she hunched her shoulders, made herself small. Still learning how to move through the world without being noticed.

I got out, the smell of gasoline and dust hitting me immediately. I unscrewed the cap and squeezed the handle, watching the numbers tick by. My eyes, however, were scanning the perimeter. Habit. Instinct.

Years of training didn't just disappear because I'd changed sides.

I checked the road behind us; empty. I checked the tree line; quiet. I checked the other cars in the lot; a rusted pickup, a sedan with a baby seat, nothing suspicious.

Then I looked at the minimart adjacent to the pumps.

My blood ran cold.

It was a faded grey utility van, the kind used for plumbing or landscaping, parked diagonally across two spots near the entrance. The rear bumper was dented, the passenger side door rusted at the hinge.

I knew that van.

I knew the dent in the bumper. Thomas had hit a pylon backing out of the compound's service yard three years ago. I'd been there. I'd watched him do it, had helped him buff out the paint transfer so the Leader wouldn't notice.

A Cult Scout.

My grip tightened on the pump handle. The rational part of my brain started calculating. How many were in the van? One? Two? Were they armed? Did they have photos of Freya, or just a description?

Thomas was competent but not exceptional. If he was alone, this would be manageable. If he had backup waiting in the van, things got complicated.

I ran through scenarios. Best case: he doesn't go inside. He gets his gas and leaves, never seeing her. Worst case: he spots her, confirms the ID, calls it in to the compound. Middle ground: he's uncertain, reports a possible sighting but can't confirm.

I could work with uncertainty. Uncertainty I could manipulate.

I squeezed the pump handle until my knuckles turned white. They were sweeping the grid. A routine patrol, looking for lost sheep who wandered off the main roads. They weren't looking for me. They were looking for runaways.

And I had one walking around inside the store.

The irony wasn't lost on me. I was supposed

to be hunting her. Instead, I was protecting her from other hunters.

Fuck.

I looked at the minimart. The sliding glass doors were open. I could see the clerk behind the counter, reading a magazine. I could see rows of chips and sodas. And then the driver's side door of the van opened.

A man stepped out. He wasn't wearing his whites, but he had the look; short hair, a stiff posture, eyes that scanned the world without really seeing it. He was a Seeker. A lower-ranking scout, but dangerous to a defector.

He stretched, rolled his shoulders, started toward the doors.

My hand drifted to my hip, to the gun holstered there. The old impulse roared in my veins, loud, violent, efficient.

I could kill him before he even reached the chip aisle. One shot to the head, drag the body behind the dumpster, drive away. Clean. Simple. Final.

The Enforcer in me wanted it. Craved the simplicity of elimination.

But killing him would cost me time. It also bought attention. Gunshots, police sirens, blood on the pavement. It would leave a trail the other scouts would follow. It would tell the Leader that I wasn't retrieving Freya; I was at war.

I needed to be a ghost. I needed to be nothing more than a rumour they weren't sure of.

I hung the nozzle back on the pump and moved. I had to get to Freya before he did.

I walked into the store, the bell dinging softly. The air smelled of coffee and floor wax. Freya was in the third aisle, looking at a wall of colourful cereal boxes. She had a box in her hands, staring at the cartoon tiger on the front like it was a religious icon.

She looked small. She looked fragile. She looked exactly like a runaway trying to remember what normal life felt like.

The Seeker was at the end of the aisle, grabbing a bottle of water. He turned.

His eyes swept past the greeting cards, past the beef jerky, and landed on her.

I saw the moment it clicked. The recognition. The way his posture shifted, the way he leaned forward to get a better look. He was seeing the girl on the missing prayer list. He was seeing the defector Father Michael wanted back.

His hand moved toward his pocket; probably reaching for a phone, or a radio.

He started toward her.

I was twenty feet away. Too far to grab him. Too far to block him physically without causing a scene. I needed him to not see her. I needed him to see something else.

I moved into the aisle, inserting myself between his line of sight and Freya. I reached out, grabbing Freya by the waist and pulling her back against me, spinning her away from the Seeker.

It looked like an intimate gesture, a lover pulling his girlfriend in for a kiss. But I positioned her body directly in front of mine, shielding her face with my shoulder.

"What?" she whispered, startled, dropping the box of cereal.

It tumbled to the floor with a hollow rattle.

"Quiet," I murmured against her ear. "Don't turn around."

I felt her tense, then force herself to relax. Smart girl. She understood we were in danger.

The Seeker stopped four feet away. His eyes were wide, confused. He looked at me, then at the back of Freya's head; all he could see of her was dark hair, a slender frame pressed against a much larger man.

"Andre?" he breathed.

The awe was thick in his voice. He thought I was on a mission. He thought I was hunting for the family.

"Thomas," I said, nodding at him. My voice was bored, dismissive. I was the Enforcer interrupted during personal time. Annoyed but not threatened. "Patrol?"

"Yes," he stammered, stepping closer, trying to peek around my arm. "Is that... is that the missing girl? The one from the—"

He cut himself off, looking around for listeners. Training kicking in. Don't discuss compound business in front of civilians.

"Not today," I said, my eyes hardening just

enough to warn him. "This is my wife. She's just tired."

I shifted my weight, tucking Freya further under my chin, making sure not a strand of her hair was visible. My heart was hammering a slow, heavy rhythm, but I kept my face slack, bored. I had to make him feel stupid for asking. I had to make him doubt his own eyes.

The lie was absurd. I'd never mentioned having a wife. But the Seekers didn't know the Enforcers' personal lives. We were shadows, weapons. We didn't have wives. We had missions.

Which made the lie just plausible enough.

The beauty of it was in the audacity. Who would be brazen enough to lie to a cult scout while standing in public view? Only someone with nothing to hide. Only someone who was exactly what he appeared to be.

The psychology was simple: people saw what they expected to see. Thomas expected the Enforcer to be hunting the girl. He did not expect the Enforcer to have turned traitor. So when presented with evidence that contradicted his expectations, his brain would work to reconcile it.

A wife explained everything. Why I looked annoyed rather than alert. Why I was protecting her rather than restraining her. Why I was in civilian clothes in a random gas station instead of in uniform at the compound.

The key was selling it with absolute confidence.

"Oh," he said, deflating. "I... I thought I recognised her. The Leader said..."

"The Leader says a lot of things," I interrupted, leaning toward him. The movement was aggressive, invading his personal space. I let the menace slip out, the Enforcer bleeding through the cracks. "You'd do well to remember your training, Thomas. Eyes forward. Mouth shut. Unless you want to explain to the Father why you're bothering his Enforcer on authorised leave?"

He blanched. The mention of the Father's name was a leash snap. He took a step back, his hands coming up in surrender.

"No. No, sir. I apologise. I... I didn't know."

"Now you do," I said. "Gas up and go home. You're chasing ghosts."

He nodded vigorously, eager to escape the conversation. He grabbed his water and practically ran for the doors. The bell dinged as he left, the sound oddly cheerful given what had just happened.

I waited until I heard the van start up. I waited until the tires crunched on the asphalt, until I heard the engine fade into the distance.

Then I let go of Freya.

She turned in my arms, looking up at me, her eyes wide and terrified. She knew. She was smart enough to know.

"He recognised me," she whispered.

"He saw a girl who looked like the one on the

poster," I corrected smoothly. I bent down and picked up the cereal box she had dropped, dusting it off. "You're fine. We need to go."

But we weren't fine. Thomas would report back. He'd mention seeing me. He'd describe the girl I was with. And even if he accepted my explanation, someone else might not.

Someone smarter. Someone who knew me better. Someone who'd put the pieces together and realise that the Enforcer had gone rogue.

The Leader would know. Maybe not today, maybe not tomorrow, but soon.

And when he knew, he'd send others. Not Seekers. Not scouts.

He'd send Enforcers.

Men I'd trained with. Men who wouldn't fall for a simple lie. Men who knew exactly how dangerous I was and would come prepared.

The clock was ticking faster now.

I walked her to the counter. I paid for the gas and the cereal, using a card instead of the cash I'd been using, just to change the routine. The clerk didn't care. He just chewed his gum and scanned the items.

We walked out to the car. The grey van was gone, just a distant dust cloud on the highway. I opened her door for her, watching her slide in. My hands were steady, but the inside of my mouth tasted like copper.

Adrenaline. Fear. The metallic tang of a close call.

I got in and started the engine.

"You didn't shoot him," she said softly as I pulled back onto the road.

I checked the mirrors. We were clear.

"No."

"Why?" she asked. She turned in her seat to look at me.

I stared at the white line marking the lane. Because if I shot him, I'd have to deal with the body. I'd have to explain the blood to the police. I'd have to deal with the next patrol they sent when he didn't check in.

Because the old me would have killed him. The Enforcer would have eliminated the witness.

The new me; the one who kept looking at her terrified, determined face, just wanted to get her away without leaving a trail of bodies behind us.

"Because he wasn't worth the cleanup," I said, which wasn't the whole truth, but was the only truth she could handle right now.

She didn't look away. She watched my profile. I felt her gaze like a touch.

"He would have taken me back," she said.

"If he knew for sure."

"Maybe," I said, gripping the wheel. "But I didn't give him the chance."

I drove faster, pushing the car up to seventy. The sun was gone now, the sky turning a bruised purple. I had almost killed a man today just to keep her hidden. And I hadn't. I had lied, I had intimidated, I had played the role of the loyal dog to get her off the leash.

I wasn't bringing her back to the Leader. I was stealing her from him.

And today, I'd decided to do it quietly.

I reached over and turned on the radio, needing noise to fill the sudden, terrifying silence in my own head. A rock song crackled through the speakers. Freya didn't object. She just leaned back and closed her eyes, her hand drifting across the console to rest near mine.

I let it stay there.

And as we drove into the darkening night, I realised something that should have terrified me but instead felt like relief: I was never going back. Not to the compound. Not to the Leader. Not to the man I'd been.

I'd crossed the line. And there was no going back.

CHAPTER 25

Freya

The safe house was a hunting cabin deep in the national forest, miles off the main road. It was isolated, quiet, the perfect place to hide. It was also the perfect place to die if we were found.

The next two weeks were a blur of training and planning. Andre didn't treat me like a child or a victim anymore. He treated me like a soldier. He taught me how to hold a knife, how to move without making a sound, how to spot a tail.

The knife lessons were the hardest. Not because of the technique; Andre was a patient teacher when he wanted to be, but because of what they represented. Every stance, every grip, every thrust was preparation for the moment when I would have to use it. On a person. On the Leader, if it came to that.

"Your hands are shaking," Andre said on

the third day, watching me practice my strikes against a leather jacket he'd hung from a tree branch.

"I'm fine."

"You're terrified." He stepped behind me, placing his hands over mine on the knife handle. "That's good. Fear keeps you alive. But you have to learn to use it, not let it use you."

I closed my eyes, feeling his warmth at my back, his breath against my ear.

"When the moment comes," he said quietly, "you won't have time to think. Your body has to remember what your mind will forget. So we practice until it's muscle memory."

We practiced until my arms ached, until the movements became automatic. Thrust, withdraw, pivot. Again. Again. The leather jacket took on the texture of flesh in my imagination, and I hated how easily that happened.

But it was the nights that changed us. There was a new intimacy between us, a raw honesty that bled into the daylight. We talked about things we had never spoken of before. I told him about the nights I couldn't remember, the flashes of white light, the feeling of hands on my neck. I told him about the guilt that gnawed at me, the feeling that I had already done terrible things for the Leader, things I couldn't recall but knew were there.

He listened, his face grim, his hand resting on my knee. He didn't tell me I was crazy. He didn't tell me to pray.

"They used hypnosis," he said, his voice tight with anger. "Drugs. Suggestions. It's not your fault, Freya."

"I feel it though," I whispered. "Like a shadow inside me."

"Then we'll kill it," he said simply. "When we kill him, we kill the shadow too."

I wanted to believe him. I wanted to believe that death could cure what had been done to me, that violence could erase the blank spaces in my memory. But a small, truthful part of me knew that some scars went too deep.

In turn, he told me more about his mother. About how she had been a drifter, addicted and beaten, until the cult found her. About how the Leader had given her purpose, a home, a reason to live.

"She calls him her saviour," Andre said, his jaw tight. "She looks at him like he's a saint."

"Maybe she needs to," I said carefully. "Maybe believing in him is easier than remembering what she was before."

He looked at me sharply. "Are you defending him?"

"No. I'm trying to understand her. Because you're going to have to face her after this, Andre. When the Leader is dead and his kingdom falls, she's going to be one of the people left standing in the ruins."

His expression darkened. "I know."

He stared into the fire for a long moment. "He's a monster. But for her, he was salvation. How do I destroy her world to save yours?"

"You don't have to destroy her world," I said, moving to sit between his legs, leaning back against his chest. "You just have to destroy the liar controlling it."

I felt him stiffen, then slowly relax. He wrapped his arms around me, burying his face in my hair.

"Sometimes I wonder if there's a difference," he murmured. "Between the man and the myth he's built. If we kill him, does his hold on them die too? Or does he become a martyr?"

"Then we make sure the truth comes out," I said. "We make sure everyone knows what he really was. The girls he hurt. The lives he destroyed. We burn down the myth along with the man."

He was quiet for a long moment, and I could feel the conflict warring inside him. The part of him that had been raised to protect the Leader versus the part that had chosen to protect me instead.

"We have to kill him," I said. It wasn't a question. It was the only way.

"I know," he said. "But he never goes anywhere without guards. The house is a fortress."

"We'll find a way," I said, turning to face him. I straddled his lap, taking his face in my hands. "We're not victims anymore, Andre. We're not little birds in a cage. We're the wolves at the door."

He looked at me, his eyes burning with fierce, possessive pride.

"You have no idea how dangerous you are."

"Show me," I challenged him, a small smile playing on my lips.

He did.

We discovered a twisted alchemy in that cabin. I began to ask for touch that once would have been forced on me. I would kneel in front of him, not because he ordered me to, but because I wanted to show him my submission. He would respond with fierce, careful attention rather than humiliation, his hands reverent on my skin. Kneeling with my hands behind my back became not an imposed shame but a posture I chose in private, one he responded to with a dark, consuming pleasure.

He, in turn, learned that control could be used to hold instead of crush. That brutality was a blade he could turn outward, toward the man who made him a weapon, instead of inward on the woman who was teaching him what consent felt like.

Afterward, lying tangled together on the narrow cot, I traced the scars on his chest with my fingertips.

"Tell me about this one," I said, touching a jagged line near his ribs.

"Training accident when I was sixteen," he said. "Another Enforcer got too enthusiastic during sparring. The Leader told me pain was a teacher."

"And this one?" A burn mark on his shoulder.

"Punishment. I questioned an order." His voice was flat, matter-of-fact. "He had me hold my arm over a candle until I apologised."

I pressed my lips to the scar, feeling him tense beneath me.

"We're going to make him pay for all of it," I whispered against his skin. "Every scar. Every girl. Every lie."

His hand came up to cradle the back of my head. "Promise me something."

"What?"

"If it goes wrong; if I don't make it out, you run. You don't look back. You don't try to save me."

I pulled back to look at him. "No."

"Freya—"

"No," I said more firmly. "We both get out, or neither of us does. Those are the only options I'm accepting."

He looked like he wanted to argue, but instead he just pulled me down into a kiss that tasted like desperation and determination in equal measure.

We planned. We mapped out the compound. He knew the patrol patterns, the blind spots. I knew the desperation of the girls inside.

The map was crude, sketched on butcher paper we'd found in the cabin's kitchen. Andre had drawn it from memory, every building, every fence line, every guard post marked with careful precision.

"The main gate has two guards at all times," he said, tapping the entrance with a pencil. "They rotate every four hours. The weakest shift is midnight to four a.m.; they're tired, less alert."

"What about cameras?"

"Three. One on the gate, one on the prayer hall, one on the Leader's house." He marked them with red X's. "But the system is old. If we cut the power—"

"They'll know something's wrong immediately," I interrupted. "We need them to think everything's normal until it's too late."

He nodded slowly. "The next gathering is in two days," Andre said, tracing the map with a finger. "The solstice ceremony. Everyone will be in the prayer hall. Even the guards."

"Everyone except the Leader?" I asked.

"He usually stays in the house," Andre said. "To pray for the ceremony. But... if there's a disturbance... if there's a fire..."

"We create a distraction," I finished. "We draw him out."

"The storage shed," Andre said, pointing to a small square on the edge of the compound. "It's full of old furniture, fabric for the costumes they use in ceremonies. It would go up fast."

"And while everyone's focused on the fire, we slip into his house."

"Through the back," Andre confirmed. "There's a door that leads directly to his private quarters. I have a key."

I stared at him. "You have a key to his bedroom?"

His expression was unreadable. "I told you. I was his favourite. He... trusted me."

The weight of what that meant hung between us. All the access the Leader had given him, all the trust he'd built over years of loyal service, and Andre was going to use every bit of it to destroy him.

"He's going to feel so betrayed," I said quietly.

"Good," Andre said, his voice hard. "Let him feel a fraction of what we've felt."

We looked at each other. The plan was suicide. It was madness.

"It's the only way," I said.

Andre nodded.

"Then we burn it down."

We spent the rest of that night refining the details. Escape routes. Contingencies. What to do if we were separated. What to say if we were caught. The questions were endless, and none of the answers felt sufficient.

As dawn began to break through the cabin windows, painting the walls in shades of gold and pink, I realised I was more afraid than I'd ever been in my life. Not afraid of dying; I'd made peace with that possibility. Afraid of failing. Afraid that we'd get so close only to have it all fall apart. Afraid that the girls still trapped in that compound would never know freedom because we weren't strong enough, smart enough, brave enough to save them.

Andre must have seen it in my face because he pulled me close, wrapping me in his arms.

"We're going to do this," he said into my hair. "We're going to burn it all down, and we're going to walk out of there together. Do you believe me?"

I wanted to. God, I wanted to.

"Ask me again after it's done," I said.

He pulled back just enough to look into my eyes. "After it's done, I'm not going to have to ask. You're going to know."

I hoped he was right. I hoped we both lived long enough to find out.

CHAPTER 26

Freya

The revelation hung in the cabin air, thick and silent. Andre had decided to burn his world for mine. He had chosen me over his mother. The weight of that choice settled over us, making the fire in the hearth seem to burn hotter, the shadows of the cabin stretch longer.

I sat on the worn rug, my back against the rough stone of the fireplace, staring at the hunting knife in my hand. The steel was cold, but my palm was sweating. The blade caught the firelight, sending small reflections dancing across the cabin walls like trapped fireflies.

I'd held knives before. In the compound kitchen, cutting vegetables for the communal meals. Under the Leader's watchful eye, learning to prepare his food exactly as he demanded. But those knives had been tools. This knife was a weapon. The difference sat heavy in my hand.

"You're thinking too loud," Andre said from the doorway.

I looked up. He was leaning against the frame, his arms crossed over his chest. He looked dangerous, but the danger was focused outward now. Not at me.

"I'm thinking about rabbits," I said, my voice sounding small in the quiet room.

"We need meat," he said. "Protein. Fat. You can't kill a man on an empty stomach, Freya."

The casualness with which he said it; kill a man, made my stomach clench. But he was right. We'd been living on canned beans and stale crackers for days. Our bodies needed real sustenance for what was coming.

"I know." I stood up, the knife handle slippery in my grip. "I'm going out."

He pushed off the doorframe.

"I'm coming with you."

"You don't have to watch."

"I know," he said. "But I'm going to."

There was something in his tone that made me understand: this wasn't about protecting me from the woods. This was about witnessing my transformation. He needed to see me cross this line, needed to know I could do what needed to be done.

We moved into the woods surrounding the cabin. The sun was beginning to dip, casting long, golden beams through the pines. It looked like a fairy tale. It felt like a trap.

The air was crisp, carrying the scent of pine sap and damp earth. Somewhere in the distance, a crow called out, harsh and mocking. My boots crunched on fallen needles, each step announcing my presence to anything that might be listening.

"Quiet," Andre murmured. "Heel to toe. Roll your weight. Like I showed you."

I adjusted my gait, trying to move the way he did; like water, like shadow. It didn't come naturally to me yet. I was still too aware of my body, too conscious of each movement.

We walked for maybe twenty minutes until the trees thinned out. The undergrowth was dense here, ferns brushing against my jeans, leaving wet trails across the denim.

"Look," Andre whispered, stopping me with a hand on my shoulder.

I froze.

"Tracks," he said, pointing to the soft mud near a fallen log.

I looked down. Small, indistinct hoof prints, barely visible in the fading light. My heart began to hammer.

"Rabbit," he said. "Fresh. It's grazing up ahead."

I swallowed hard. My stomach turned over.

"Okay."

"Freya." He turned me to face him, his hands on my shoulders. "You see that rabbit, you see the

Leader."

I blinked.

"What?"

"It's the same instinct," he said, his eyes dark and serious. "The rabbit is a threat to your survival. You can't hesitate. You can't feel guilty. You strike to end."

The compound had taught me that all life was sacred. That taking life, even an animal's, required prayer and penance. That we were stewards of creation, not its destroyers. But Andre was teaching me something different. He was teaching me that my life had value too. That survival wasn't a sin.

"I know," I said, but the tremor was in my hands.

"Do you?" He studied my face. "Because when we walk into that compound, when you see him standing there in his white robes looking like a saint, you can't remember the prayers he taught you. You can't remember the man he pretended to be. You have to remember what he is."

"A predator."

"Exactly. And what do you do with predators?"

"You kill them before they kill you."

He nodded, satisfied. "Show me," he said.

We moved forward, stepping quietly. He moved like a ghost, making no sound. I tried to mimic him, placing my feet carefully, breathing through my nose. My senses sharpened. The world narrowed to sound and scent and the whisper of my own pulse in my ears.

Every rustle made my heart skip. A bird taking flight. A squirrel chattering above. The forest was alive with movement, but I was learning to distinguish what mattered from what didn't. Andre had taught me that; to filter the noise, to focus on the prey.

"There," he breathed, barely audible. His finger pointed through a gap in the ferns.

Then, I saw it.

It was about twenty yards away. A brown rabbit, fat and healthy, nibbling on a patch of clover near a stump. It twitched its nose, innocent. Alive. Its fur gleamed in the dying light, ears swiveling to catch sounds I couldn't hear.

My breath hitched. It looked soft. It looked like a creature that deserved to live, not die in the mud.

For a moment, I was back in the compound garden, watching the rabbits that lived in the hutches behind the prayer hall. We'd been taught to care for them, to feed them, to see them as God's creatures entrusted to our stewardship. I remembered stroking their soft ears, feeling their rapid heartbeats under my palm.

I remembered the day the Leader had one slaughtered for a feast. How he'd made us all watch. How he'd said it was a lesson in the cycle of life and death, in our dominion over lesser creatures. I'd been twelve and I'd cried for days.

Now here I was, knife in hand, preparing to do the same thing.

"I can't," I whispered.

"You have to," Andre said in my ear, his breath warm against my neck. "You're going to kill him. You're going to be grateful he gave his life so you can keep yours."

I felt sick. The compound's teachings warred with my instincts, the reverence for life, the guilt of taking it. But Andre was telling me to embrace the killer inside me. To accept that I could be both; the girl who valued life and the woman who would take it to survive.

"I don't have a gun," I said, my voice rising in panic. "I have to get close."

"Then be quiet," he said. "Be fast."

I started forward, my whole body trembling. Each step felt like walking through water. The rabbit's ears twitched, but it kept eating, unaware that death was creeping toward it on shaking legs.

Ten yards. Eight. Six.

The wind shifted. The rabbit's head snapped up. It saw me. It didn't run immediately, just stared, trying to assess the threat.

"Move," Andre commanded, a low growl that vibrated in my chest.

I launched myself. I didn't think about Elara. I didn't think about the prayer hall. I just ran. I crashed through the ferns, my boots slamming into the earth. The rabbit bolted. It was fast, a blur of brown fur, zig-zagging toward a hollow log.

My lungs burned. My legs screamed. But I was faster than I'd ever been, fuelled by adrenaline and desperation and two weeks of training. I scrambled over the deadfall, gaining on it. The distance closed in seconds.

I threw myself at it. I didn't use the knife yet, just my weight. I slammed it down into the leaves. It thrashed under me, powerful hind legs kicking at my stomach. The breath left me in a rush. Sharp claws raked at my forearms, stinging like fire. I gasped, scrambling to find purchase on the slippery fur.

It was screaming; a high, terrified sound that hurt my ears. A sound I'd heard before, in my own throat, in the throats of other girls.

"Do it!" Andre shouted from behind me. "End it!"

I gripped the scruff of its neck with my left hand, pinning it down. Its eyes bulged, wide and wild. It looked at me with pure fear.

I raised the knife. My hand shook so hard the blade wobbled.

The rabbit's heart hammered against my palm, a frantic drumbeat.

Thump-thump-thump.

It's innocent. It's just eating. It didn't do anything wrong.

It's the Leader. Kill it before it kills you.

I thought about white robes soaked in blood.

I thought about Elara's vacant eyes. I thought about the belt around my throat and the way he'd smiled while I choked.

I slammed the knife down.

The blade struck just behind the ear, where Andre had taught me. Clean. Quick. The rabbit stiffened, then went limp. The scream cut off instantly.

I yanked the knife out, scrambling back, breathing in ragged gasps. My hands were shaking so violently I dropped the knife in the dirt. I looked down. The rabbit lay on its side, blood soaking into the leaves. It was just meat now. Just food.

The silence of the woods rushed back in. Birds resumed their songs. The wind stirred the branches. The world continued, indifferent to the small death I'd just caused.

I stared at it, waiting for the remorse, the nausea, the crushing guilt the compound promised would come to sinners.

Nothing came.

I stared at the blood, and the only thing I felt was relief. I was alive. I won.

But there was something else too. Something that scared me more than the killing itself. I felt powerful. For the first time in my life, I had decided when something lived or died. Not the Leader. Not God. Me.

The compound had taught me I was nothing. A vessel. A tool. My body didn't belong to me; it belonged to the community, to the Leader, to the cause. My choices weren't mine. My life wasn't mine.

But this kill was mine. I chose it. I executed it. And the world didn't end. Lightning didn't strike me down. I wasn't damned.

I was just a girl with blood on her hands and air in her lungs.

I dropped to my knees in the dirt, covering my face with my hands. I started to cry, not for the rabbit, but for the girl who had been too afraid to kill to survive. That girl was gone now. In her place was someone harder. Someone dangerous.

Footsteps crunched on the leaves. I looked up. Andre stood over me. He didn't look disappointed. He didn't look disgusted. He looked proud.

"Get up, Freya," he said, reaching down a hand. "You did good."

I took his hand and let him pull me up. My knees wobbled, but I didn't fall.

"I killed it," I said, wiping my nose on my sleeve.

"Yes," he said. He looked down at the rabbit, then back at me. "And you didn't die."

He pulled a bandana from his pocket and wiped the blood from my cheek; blood I hadn't even realised was there.

"Remember this feeling," he said softly, his thumb brushing my skin. "When you face him.

It's just survival. It's just meat."

I looked at the rabbit again. The guilt was still a faint echo, but it was fading. Buried under it was something harder. Something sharp.

I could kill. I could take a life to save my own.

I looked at Andre, at the hard line of his jaw, at the gun at his hip.

"I'll do it," I said, my voice gaining strength. "When we go there. I won't hesitate."

"I know," he said. He squeezed my hand, then let go. "Pick it up. We're eating tonight."

I picked up the rabbit by its hind legs. The weight was warm. Heavy. The fur was soft under my fingers, still carrying the heat of life.

We walked back to the cabin in the twilight, a predator and her mate carrying the corpse of the forest. The animal was dead, but I had never felt more alive.

Behind us, the last light caught on the blood trail we'd left, painting the leaves red. Like bread-crumbs marking the path from who I was to who I was becoming.

CHAPTER 27

Freya

The morning we left the cabin, the air smelled different. The scent of pine and woodsmoke, which had wrapped us in a blanket of safety for days, was replaced by the smell of damp earth and impending violence. The rain had finally stopped, but the sky remained a heavy, bruised grey, pressing down on us as if trying to hold us in place.

I stood on the porch for a moment, breathing in that strange air. Behind me, I could hear Andre moving through the cabin one last time, checking for anything we might have forgotten. But I knew we weren't forgetting anything. We were leaving this place deliberately, walking away from the only peace either of us had ever known.

The cabin had become more than shelter. It had been a chrysalis, a space between what we were and what we were becoming. Here, in these four walls, the Enforcer had learned to be gentle. The captive had learned to be dangerous. We'd transformed each other in ways neither of us had planned.

I thought about the nights we'd spent here. The quiet conversations by the fire. The way he'd taught me to clean a gun, his hands steady on mine. The morning I'd killed the rabbit and he'd looked at me with something that might have been pride. The hours spent planning, mapping, preparing for this moment.

We'd been playing house, I realised. Pretending we were normal people with a normal future. Cooking meals. Sleeping in each other's arms. Making love like we had all the time in the world.

But the clock had been ticking the whole time. And now it had run out.

We packed in silence. There wasn't much to take; just the clothes on our backs, the weapons we'd cleaned, the map we'd drawn on butcher paper. Andre moved around the room, checking corners, sweeping for anything we might have left behind. He looked bigger in the small space, his broad shoulders blocking the light. He was the Enforcer again. The lover who had held me in the night was gone, buried under the soldier walking us back into hell.

I watched him work, noting the shift in his posture, the set of his jaw. This was the man who'd hunted me through the woods. The predator. Not the person who'd whispered my name in the dark, who'd taught me that control could be a gift instead of a weapon.

Both versions were real. Both were true. I was learning that people could be multiple things at once.

"We need supplies," Andre said, slinging the bag over his shoulder. "Fuel. Oil. Food."

I nodded, pulling my hood low.

"Okay."

I took one last look around the cabin. The fireplace where we'd cooked our simple meals. The floor where he'd taught me to fight. The bed where we'd discovered what it meant to choose each other, again and again, despite everything.

"Ready?" Andre asked from the doorway.

Was I ready to leave safety? To walk back into the nightmare we'd escaped?

No. But I was willing.

"Yeah," I said. "Let's go."

We walked out to the car. The gravel crunched under our boots, a sound that felt too loud in the quiet of the forest. I looked back at the cabin once. The windows were dark eyes staring back at me. For two weeks, it had been a home. The only home I'd ever known where I wasn't afraid.

Now, I was afraid again. But it was a different kind of fear. Not the paralyzed terror of the compound, but the sharp, focused fear of a predator preparing to strike.

We drove for an hour, leaving the deep

woods and hitting the highway. The closer we got to the compound's location, the more tense Andre became. His knuckles were white on the steering wheel, his jaw set in a hard line.

I watched the landscape change outside my window. The dense forest giving way to cleared land, farms, signs of civilisation. Each mile marker felt like a countdown. Each passing car might contain someone who recognised us, who'd report back to the Leader. The paranoia was a living thing, coiled in my chest.

He pulled into a gas station attached to a small convenience store. It was bright, fluorescent, mundane. The kind of place where normal people stopped for cigarettes and lottery tickets and bags of chips. The kind of place where people like us; people planning murder, shouldn't exist.

"Stay in the car," he said, cutting the engine. "I'll be fast."

"I want to come," I said quickly. I hated being left alone. The vulnerability of sitting in a parked car, visible, exposed, made my skin crawl. "I need... I need to use my legs."

He looked at me, his eyes scanning my face. He seemed to see the desperation there, the restlessness. The way sitting still made me feel like prey.

"Fine," he said. "But you stay close. And you keep your head down."

We went inside. The air smelled of stale coffee and floor wax. It was a sensory assault after the clean, sharp air of the mountains. Fluorescent lights buzzed overhead, too bright, too harsh. A radio played tinny country music. An old woman was comparing prices on canned soup.

Normal. Everything was so aggressively normal.

I walked close to Andre, his presence a shield that kept the world at bay. He moved to the counter. I stood a few feet away, looking at a rack of beef jerky. My hands were trembling slightly, so I shoved them into my pockets.

I tried to look casual, just another customer browsing. But I felt like I was wearing a sign: MURDERER. RUNAWAY. DANGER.

I watched him. To me, he was just Andre. The man who had bandaged my feet. The man who had kissed me in the rain. But as he stood at the counter, his back to me, I saw how the rest of the world saw him.

The clerk was a bored teenage boy, chewing gum and reading a magazine. He didn't look up until Andre's shadow fell over him.

Then the boy looked up. And froze.

The colour drained from his face. He stopped chewing. He stared at Andre's jacket, at the way he stood, at the sheer size of him. He looked like a rabbit that had just scented a wolf.

Andre placed three boxes of ammo on the counter, along with bottles of water, cans of oil, and a stack of protein bars. He didn't speak. He just looked at the kid.

The silence stretched. The boy's hands shook as he scanned the items. His eyes kept darting to the door, to the phone, to the silent alarm under the counter.

"I... I need ID for... for the ammo," the boy stammered, his voice cracking.

Andre didn't move. He didn't reach for his wallet. He just looked at the boy. It was a look of absolute, bored dismissal. A look that said, I can kill you before your hand even touches that button.

The boy swallowed hard, his Adam's apple bobbing.

"I... I guess it's okay. Just... just this once."

Andre dropped a crumpled wad of cash on the counter. He didn't wait for the change. He just grabbed the bags and turned.

"Let's go," he said to me.

I followed him out, the cold air hitting my face. I felt the eyes of the clerk on my back, burning like laser pointers. I felt the fear he radiated, a dark aura that screamed danger.

I got into the car, my heart racing. I looked over at Andre as he started the engine.

"He was terrified of you," I whispered.

Andre checked the mirrors, merging onto the road.

"Good."

"He thought you were going to kill him," I said.

Andre glanced at me, his face hard.

"I didn't kill him."

"No," I said. "But you wanted to."

His hands tightened on the wheel. For a moment, I thought he'd deny it. But this was the new honesty we'd built between us. No more lies.

"I did what I had to do," he said, his voice rough. "To get us out. To get back to the work."

The work. Murder. Assassination. Burning down everything the Leader had built.

When had that become our work?

He didn't speak for the rest of the drive. The silence was heavy, filled with the things we weren't saying. We were going to the compound. We were going to kill. And the boy at the gas station was just the first person who would look at us and know something was wrong.

I wondered if we'd ever be able to go back to normal. If there was a version of the future where we could walk into a gas station without radiating threat, where we could exist in the world without people flinching.

I didn't think so. We'd crossed too many lines. Become too dangerous.

We drove for another twenty minutes. The landscape became familiar. The twisted pines. The rocky outcrops. I felt my chest tighten with every mile, the old anxiety pressing against my ribs like a live thing.

Then, I saw it. The neon sign buzzing in the twilight. Vacancy.

I knew the curve of the road. I knew the peeling paint on the railing outside the second floor.

Andre slowed the car, turning into the lot.

"You remember this place?" he asked.

"This is it," I whispered. "This is where I stayed."

My throat went dry. This was Room 104. This was where I had showered for the first time without a timer. Where I had wept because the world was overwhelming and cruel. Where I had come back to find the symbol carved into my door. Where he had caught me.

The memory was so vivid it made my chest ache. I could still remember the feeling of seeing that symbol; the shock, the betrayal, the realisation that I'd never really been free at all. That even my small rebellion, my tiny taste of independence, had been watched. Monitored. Allowed.

I'd thought I was flying. I'd been on a leash the whole time.

He parked the car right out front.

"I thought this would be fitting," he said quietly. "Seeing as we are coming full circle."

A smile crossed his lips, ironic and quiet.

I looked at the room. The door was visible from the car. The wood was darkened by rain and weather, but I could see the jagged gouges in the center. The circle. The four points. The symbol was still there. A scar on the door, a brand that hadn't faded.

I had run from this place, terrified and bleeding. He had dragged me back from here, a captive in chains. And now we were back.

"Makes sense," I said, opening the door.

The air outside smelled of wet asphalt and pine, but it was the same air I had breathed when I thought I was free.

We walked to the room. My steps felt heavy, dragging against the pavement. Andre was right; it did feel like coming full circle. I had run away, thinking I was flying to a new life. I had been caught, dragged back, and broken. And now, I was returning to the start, ready to burn it all down.

We stopped at the door. Andre reached out and touched the rough wood, his fingers tracing the deep cuts of the compass. Four points.

"Loyalty. Perfection. Worship. Truth," I murmured.

The words that had defined my entire life. The prison bars disguised as virtues.

Andre looked at me, his eyes dark.

"Not anymore."

"Not anymore," I agreed.

He unlocked the door. It swung open, the same heavy creak I remembered. We stepped inside.

The room was small, dingy, and perfect. It smelled of stale smoke and old carpet. I looked at the bed where I had huddled under the sheets, listening to the hum of the ice machine down the walkway. I looked at the bathroom door where I had bandaged my own feet.

Every surface held a memory. Every corner whispered of the girl I'd been.

I turned to Andre. He was already unloading the supplies, placing the oil and the bullets on the dresser with a heavy clatter. He looked at me, then at the empty doorframe, then back at me.

"It's just a place," he said, his voice low. "It doesn't have any power over you."

"I know," I said. "But it remembers."

And so did I. I remembered the terror. The exhaustion. The desperate hope that had died when I saw the symbol carved into my door.

But I also remembered what came after. The training. The transformation. The choice to become something other than a victim.

He walked over to me, stopping in the center of the room. He reached out, his hand cupping the back of my neck, his thumb brushing my jaw.

"We end it here," he said. "Tomorrow night, we will go back and we will finish it."

I leaned into his touch, feeling the callus on his palm, the gun oil and the soap. I looked at the door, at the symbol carved into it. I wasn't the girl who had run from this room anymore. I wasn't the victim who had been dragged back here.

"We end it," I said.

And this time, when I walked over to the bed to sit, I didn't feel like a caged bird. I felt like a wolf checking her den before the hunt.

CHAPTER 28

Freya

You will become one with us all.

It was the first thing I heard, even before the sound of my own breathing.

I lay still, staring at the ceiling of the cheap motel room. The water stain above the bed looked like a face in the dim pre-dawn light; hollow eyes, gaping mouth. Screaming or praying, I couldn't tell which. Maybe there was no difference.

Andre was already awake, standing by the window, looking out at the grey dawn. He was checking his weapons again, the slide of the gun, the rasp of the knife against the whetstone. The rhythmic sound should have been soothing, but it only made my pulse hammer faster.

This was it. The day we either freed ourselves or died trying.

I watched him, and the shame came, as it

always did now. Not shame for the acts themselves; the roughness, the pain he inflicted on me, the way he held me down until I shattered, but a twisted, confusing guilt for the fact that I didn't feel shame for liking it. I should feel degraded. I should feel used. That was what the cult taught me, that the body was a vessel to be kept pure, that desire was corruption.

But with Andre, the pain and domination didn't shatter me; they soothed me. They anchored me in the present, chasing away the ghosts of the white room. When he used his strength to control me, I didn't feel like a victim. I felt like I existed.

He turned from the window, his eyes finding mine in the dim light. He looked tired, haunted by the knowledge of what he had to do. He had confessed to me last night, his voice rough with self-loathing, about the girls he had watched walk into the Leader's house. He had stood by while they were remade into obedient shells. He was carrying the weight of every blank stare, every broken mind.

"How long have you been awake?" I asked, my voice rough with sleep.

"Long enough."

"Nightmares?"

"Memories," he corrected. "Which might be worse."

I sat up, letting the sheet pool around my waist. The air was cold against my skin, raising goosebumps. "Tell me."

He set down the whetstone, the knife catching the weak dawn light. "I keep seeing their faces. All the girls I brought back over the years. All the ones I delivered to him." His jaw clenched. "I told myself I was protecting them. Bringing them home. But I was just... feeding them to a monster."

"You were surviving," I said softly. "We all were."

"That's not good enough anymore."

"No," I agreed. "It's not."

"Ready?" he asked, though we both knew there was no such thing as ready for what we were about to do.

I sat up, the sheet falling away. My body was a map of our training; bruises fading from purple to yellow, muscles sore but strong in ways they'd never been before. I was harder now. Sharper. The cult had tried to make me soft and pliable, something to be moulded. Andre had taught me to be steel.

I checked the knife strapped to my thigh; Andre had taught me how to secure it so it wouldn't shift or cut me when I moved. The leather was soft against my skin now, broken in from practice. I checked the small pistol tucked into the waistband of my jeans. The weight of it was still foreign, but my hands knew how to hold it, how to aim, how to breathe through the kick.

"Remember," Andre said, watching me check

my weapons, "the gun is a last resort. If you fire it, everyone knows where we are."

"I remember."

"And if we get separated—"

"We meet at the old oak tree by the southern fence," I recited. We'd gone over the plan a hundred times. "If you're not there in thirty minutes, I assume you're dead or captured and I run."

"And you don't come back for me."

"Don't ask me to promise that," I said quietly.

His expression softened. "Freya—"

"I won't leave you there," I interrupted. "Just like you wouldn't leave me. So let's make sure it doesn't come to that."

Andre crossed the room and knelt in front of me, his hands settling on my knees. "We always have a choice, Freya. We could run. We could disappear. Change our names, go somewhere he'd never find us."

"And leave everyone else behind?" I shook my head. "Leave Valerie and the others? Leave all those girls in that house?"

"They might not want to be saved."

"I didn't want to be saved either, at first," I reminded him. "But you saved me anyway."

Something flickered in his eyes; pain, pride, love. He leaned forward and pressed his forehead to mine.

"If this goes wrong—"

"It won't."

"If it does," he insisted, "I need you to run.

Promise me you'll run."

"Only if you promise the same thing."

He pulled back, a ghost of a smile on his lips. "Deal."

We moved out at dawn. The plan was soaked in risk, a suicide mission wrapped in a cloak of desperation. We didn't go through the main gates. We used the river route, the same gap in the fence I had escaped through weeks ago.

The water was freezing, biting at my skin, but it felt like a baptism of a different kind. The current pulled at my legs, trying to drag me downstream, but I pushed against it. This time I wasn't running away. This time I was running toward.

When we hauled ourselves out onto the muddy bank, the compound was quiet. The peace of the garden, the neatly tended beds, it was all a lie. A pretty forest veneer painted over a rotting structure.

I stood there dripping, looking at the place that had been my entire world for eighteen months. The cabins where I'd slept. The prayer hall where I'd knelt until my knees bled. The garden where I'd pulled weeds and pretended that obedience would keep me safe.

It looked smaller now. Less imposing. Just buildings and dirt and lies.

"You okay?" Andre whispered.

"I'm home," I said, and the word tasted bitter. "Let's burn it down."

We moved toward the main buildings. Andre had planted a small device on the far side of the compound before we left. The distraction was due to go off in about an hour, but we needed to be in position before the chaos started.

The morning air smelled of dew and earth and something else; something sour that might have been fear or might have just been me. My boots squelched in the mud. Too loud. Every sound felt amplified, like the compound itself was listening.

We were intercepted near the dining hall. It wasn't the guards who came first. It was the women. A dozen of them stepped out from between the cabins, appearing like ghosts in their pastel shifts. They were dressed in their morning prayer clothes, their hair neatly pinned. I recognised them. I had eaten beside them. I had worked in the gardens with them. I had shared their prayers and their silences and their fear.

Valerie was at the front.

"Freya," she said, her face lighting up with a smile that didn't reach her eyes. "You've returned. We were watching the gates, but you never came through. The guards said you were lost to the world."

She looked at my wet clothes, the mud caked on my legs, and then at Andre. She was confused, but she wasn't angry. She thought he had done his job. She thought he was bringing the stray home.

"We took the river," Andre said, his voice tight. "It was faster."

Valerie nodded, accepting this with the easy credulity of someone who'd been taught never to question.

"The Father will be pleased that you are back. He has prepared a ceremony. But you are dirty, Freya. You should wash before you approach the house." She stepped forward, reaching out to take my arm, to guide me like a lost child. "You are safe now. The Enforcer has brought you home."

The words hit me like a physical blow. Home. As if this place of cages and lies could ever be home. As if safety could exist in a place where your mind belonged to someone else.

Andre and I exchanged a glance. This was it. The masquerade was over.

"I'm not here for a ceremony, Val," I said softly.

I reached down and pulled the knife Andre had given me. The blade flashed in the morning light. Valerie froze, her eyes widening as the metal glinted.

"Freya? What..."

Before she could finish, Andre raised his gun. He didn't aim it at her, not yet, but he racked the slide with a sharp clack that echoed like a gunshot in the quiet yard. The women gasped as one, a collective intake of breath. They looked from the gun to Andre, confusion warring with their conditioning.

"Andre?" Valerie's voice wavered. She looked at the weapon, then at his face, expecting to see a threat to me, or a warning to them. She didn't understand. "You caught her. You brought her back. Why the gun? Put it down. She needs re-integration, not a weapon."

"He's not taking me to the house for reintegration," I said, my voice gaining strength. "We're here for the Leader."

The air shifted instantly. The confusion curdled into something darker. They weren't just looking at a captive anymore; they were looking at a threat.

"You're here to cleanse her," Valerie said, her voice hardening, stepping between me and the path to the hill. "Father Michael loves us. We will protect him."

"He doesn't love you," I said, and the truth of it broke something in my chest. "He owns you. There's a difference."

"He's here to destroy you," Andre said, his voice low and dangerous. "Stand down, Valerie."

They moved as one. The violence in the compound spilled from psychological into physical in a heartbeat. The pretty veneer bled. They didn't have weapons, but they had numbers and a madness that knew no pain. They came at us with fingers curled into claws, with teeth bared, screaming prayers that sounded like curses. They were defending their cage with the ferocity of the trapped.

The explosion tore through the morning like the hand of God ripping the sky open. The storage shed on the far side of the compound erupted in a plume of orange fire that turned the early dawn into day. The concussive force hit us in a wave, a pressure that squeezed the air from our lungs and rattled our bones. For one suspended heartbeat, everything stopped. The screaming stopped. The clawing stopped. Every head turned toward the fireball climbing into the sky, eyes wide and blank with animal terror.

In that moment of shocked stillness, we moved. Andre grabbed my arm and hauled me forward through the frozen tableau of bodies. The spell broke almost immediately; confused shouts, someone screaming about demons, about judgment, but the madness had fractured. They were no longer one organism moving with singular purpose. They scattered, some running toward the fire, others away from it, a few still reaching for us but with hesitation now, with fear.

We had our opening.

I fought. I used the moves Andre had taught me in the woods. I struck out, kicked, shoved, but I couldn't bring myself to use the knife on them. They were victims. They were the hollow shells Andre had described; my friends, my sisters, turned into weapons by the man we were going to kill.

"Freya, watch out!"

A girl leaped at me, wrapping her hands around my throat. Her grip was surprisingly strong, her eyes wide and unseeing. I recognised her; Sarah, who used to braid my hair during evening prayer. Sweet Sarah who cried when the rabbits died.

I clawed at her face, panic rising. I couldn't breathe.

Andre was there. He tore the girl off me, throwing her into the dirt. But he didn't hurt her. He couldn't.

"Stop!" he roared, his voice cracking over the courtyard. "Look at you! You're fighting for your chains! Look at what he's done to you!"

He grabbed another woman by the shoulder, spinning her away from me, but instead of striking, he shoved her back, trying to create space.

"He didn't save you!" he shouted at Valerie, who was circling us like a wolf. "He erased you!"

"We are at peace!" Valerie screamed back, her face twisting in fanatical rage. "You are the demon! You are the defiler!"

They were too far gone. The mind control had twisted their devotion into feral aggression. We had to fight our way through them, leaving them groaning on the ground, bruised and broken, to get to the house.

My chest heaved as we climbed. Each step felt heavier than the last. Behind us, the women were picking themselves up, some crying, some still shouting prayers. None of them understanding that we were trying to free them.

We reached the top of the hill, breathless and bleeding. I had a scratch on my cheek from a jagged fingernail; Andre's knuckles were split. The women lay scattered behind us on the slope.

The door to the Leader's house was locked. I stepped aside. Andre moved forward with a paper clip in his hand; a skill he'd learned as a boy, he'd told me, back when locks were the only thing standing between him and food.

He carefully worked it around the lock until it clicked open.

The sound was so small. So ordinary. But it felt like the world breaking in half.

We burst inside, weapons raised. The house was silent, a stark contrast to the chaos outside. We moved through the hallway, checking the rooms.

Everything was exactly as I remembered. The photographs on the walls; the Leader surrounded by his followers, smiling like a benevolent father. The furniture, simple but expensive. The smell of sandalwood incense and something underneath it. Something rotten.

We found him in the study.

CHAPTER 29

Andre

Father Michael was standing by the fireplace, his back to us. He seemed to be staring at the portrait of himself that hung over the mantle, admiring the brushstrokes as if they were holy scripture. The room was thick with silence, a heavy, opulent quiet that blocked out the sounds of the fight still echoing in my head. The room was soundproof, a sanctuary where he couldn't hear the screams of the guards or the frantic pulse of the cult.

He didn't turn around. He just stood there, bathed in the golden light of the fire.

"You are late," he said softly. His voice carried that familiar cadence, the smooth oil over water that had commanded my life for twenty years. "I expected you two hours ago. The perimeter alarms indicated an intruder, yet you took your time. I hope you handled the disruption with efficiency."

I raised my gun. The weight of it was familiar, but the aim felt foreign. My hands were steady, but my heart was hammering against my ribs.

"Turn around, Father."

The old man turned. He didn't move quickly, or with fear. He turned with a slow, deliberate grace, the heavy robes settling around him. He didn't look at the gun in my hand. He looked at me with the same disappointed benevolence he had worn the day he gave me the bracelet; the day he told me I was his sword.

"Hello, Freya," he said, his eyes shifting to her, warm and possessive. "I see you have returned. I forgive you of your tantrum. Running is a sickness of the spirit, but I see you have brought yourself back for healing. Surrender is the first step toward salvation." He turned his gaze back to me. "And you, Andre. My most faithful dog." A small, sad smile touched his lips. "I expected this from her. She is weak. She is flawed. The world has infected her with chaotic thoughts. But you? You were raised in these walls. You drank the milk of our truth. To raise a hand against me is to raise a hand against your own mother."

"I saw what you did to them," I said, my voice trembling with rage I couldn't quite suppress. The image of the hollow-eyed girls flashed behind my eyes. "I saw the room. The chair. The lights."

Father Michael sighed, shaking his head slowly.

"The necessary tools of correction."

"No," I spat, stepping closer, the muzzle of the gun drifting toward his chest. "I saw the hypnosis. You didn't save them. You erased them. You cut them out and filled them with yourself until they were nothing but echoes."

"They were in pain," he said, his voice dropping into a soothing, hypnotic register. "They were lost. I gave them peace. I took away their confusion, their fear, their burdens. Just as I gave your mother peace."

As if summoned by her name, a figure appeared in the doorway behind him. My breath caught in my throat. It was my mother. She was wearing her white prayer dress, the fabric stark against the pale skin of her throat. Her hands were clasped loosely in front of her, her posture one of absolute submission.

"Andre?" she whispered, her eyes widening as they took in the scene; the gun, the rage, the tension. She didn't look at the gun, really. She looked at my face, seeing the betrayal there. "What are you doing?"

The sound of her voice was a knife in my gut. It wasn't fear for her life. It was fear for my soul.

"Put the gun down, Andre," she pleaded, stepping forward, her hands trembling. "You're frightening Father Michael. You're frightening me. This isn't obedience. This isn't love."

"Love?" I shouted, the word tearing out of me. "You call this love? You're a shell, Mother! You're what he made you!"

She flinched as if I had struck her.

"I am whole," she said, her voice gaining strength from the belief. "I am saved. And you are throwing it away."

"Put the gun down, son," Father Michael said, echoing her, his voice calm. Unbothered. "Look at her. Look at the peace I gave her. You want to destroy that?"

I looked at my mother. I saw the serenity on her face, the lack of lines around her eyes, the emptiness that she mistook for grace. I looked at Freya, standing behind me, bruised and battered, but blazing with a life that terrified me. I looked back at my mother.

"I am not your dog," I whispered.

"Andre, please," she said, a tear sliding down her cheek. "Don't let the devil win."

"The devil is already here," I said, the gun steady. "And he's wearing a white robe."

"Father Michael is our shepherd," she said, stepping further into the room. There was a frantic edge to her voice now, a terrifying devotion. "How dare you threaten him. Kneel, Andre! Kneel and ask for forgiveness!"

She moved toward me, her hands raised. The Leader smiled. A small, cold curve of his lips. My jaw tightened. I looked at Freya, agony written in every line of my face. I couldn't fight my mother. And I couldn't let her stop us. She saw the decision in my eyes.

I lowered the gun slightly, reaching for the tranquiliser syringe in my pocket; something we had brought as a non-lethal option.

"I'm sorry," I whispered.

I moved faster than I ever knew I could. I dodged her grasping hands, wrapping her in a bear hug, pinning her arms to her sides. She screamed, a high, terrible sound, fighting me with the strength of a madwoman.

"Forgive him!" she shrieked at the ceiling. "Punish him!"

I pressed the syringe into her neck. Her struggling slowed, then stopped. I lowered her gently to the floor, brushing the hair away from her face. She looked peaceful now, her hostility vanished into a drugged sleep. It broke me. Fractured my soul. I had sedated my own mother for a cause she hated me for.

"End it," I said, my voice hollow. I kept my gun trained on the door, guarding her back. "Freya. End it."

I looked at the Leader. He was watching me with mild interest, as if this were just another fascinating drama in his play.

"He will never forgive you," the Leader said to Freya. "You have turned his mother against him. You have corrupted the faithful."

She walked toward him, the heavy knife in

her hand. Her hand was steady.

"I'm not the one who corrupted them," Freya said. "You hollowed them out."

"Killing me won't change who you are," he said, his eyes locking onto hers. "You will always be the girl who ran. The girl who needs to be controlled."

She stopped in front of him and raised the knife.

"You're wrong," she said. "I'm the girl who learned how to bite back."

She drove the knife into his chest. It wasn't a graceful kill. It was brutal. His eyes widened in genuine surprise, perhaps for the first time in his life. He was looking at the girl he thought he had broken, realising too late that he had only forged her into something sharper. She pulled the knife out and stabbed him again. And again. She didn't hesitate. She didn't stop to ask for forgiveness, or to pray, or to beg for mercy. She just kept driving the steel into him, her face a mask of fierce, beautiful retribution.

He slumped against the mantle, sliding down to the floor. The blood soaked into his pristine white robes, staining them red.

She stepped back, dropping the knife. Her hands were covered in him. She looked down at the body.

I waited for her to collapse, waited for the horror, the nausea, the crushing guilt the cult had promised would come to those who sinned against the father. But it didn't come. Instead, an eerie calm settled over her. The room was quiet. The world felt balanced. The scale had tipped back.

Pride swelled in my chest.

She looked at me, a strange look on her face.

"Freya?" I asked, stepping over the body to get to her.

"I feel... okay," she whispered. "I don't feel guilty, Andre. Does that make me a monster?"

"No," I said, coming to her. I took her bloody hands in mine, not caring that it stained me too. "It makes you free. I'm so proud of you, little bird."

I looked down at her hands, then back at her face. The only guilt she felt was for the absence of it. She felt guilty for not feeling guilty. She had killed a monster, and all she felt was relief.

Then, a gunshot shattered the calm. The bullet slammed into the bookshelf behind her, showering us with splinters of wood. I didn't think, I just moved. I shoved her behind me, twisting to shield her body with mine.

We spun around. Standing in the doorway was the Leader's son. He looked like his father; tall, blond, handsome, with the same dead eyes. He raised a rifle, aiming at me.

"You thought it would be that easy?" he spat, his voice dripping venom. "You thought you could just kill the king and the kingdom would fall?"

"Run, Freya!" I shoved her toward the side exit. Another shot rang out. The impact hit me like a sledgehammer, slamming into my shoulder. I grunted, stumbling back, blood blooming instantly on my shirt.

"Andre!" she screamed, stopping.

"I'm fine! Go!"

She grabbed my arm, dragging me toward the door. We burst out onto the porch. The compound below was in chaos; smoke rising from the sheds, people running, screaming.

"Kill them!" the son roared from inside the house. "Bring them back to me!"

More guards were coming up the hill. We didn't have a choice. We couldn't fight them all.

"Go!" I shouted, pushing her ahead of me. "To the trees!"

We ran toward the tree line, away from the house, away from the river. Bullets kicked up dirt around our feet, thudding into the trees. I ignored the fire in my shoulder, the blood soaking my sleeve. All that mattered was the girl in front of me. We scrambled down the steep incline at the back of the property, tearing through brambles, ignoring the slashes on our skin. I was weak from the gunshot wound, my breathing ragged, but I kept moving, forcing my legs to work.

We hit the forest floor, sprinting for the cover of the deep woods. Behind us, on the hill, I saw the son standing on the porch. He wasn't chasing us. He was just watching. Even from this distance, I could hear his voice carrying over the wind, cold and certain.

"You can run!" he screamed. "But you will never be free! I will take up my father's task! You will become one with us all!"

We didn't stop until the compound was miles behind us, until the only sounds were the wind in the trees and our own ragged gasps. We collapsed against the roots of a massive oak tree, hidden in the shadows. I slid down the bark, clutching my shoulder. I was pale, losing blood, but I was alive. Freya was bruised, bleeding, covered in the Leader's blood.

But we were alive.

I looked at Freya, then back toward the compound. The phrase hung in the air like smoke. You will become one with us all. I leaned my head back against the rough bark. The son had taken up the mantle. The cult wasn't dead. It had just evolved.

We weren't free. Not yet. But for the first time, we were fighting on our own terms.

CHAPTER 30

Freya

When we got back to the motel, we didn't stay. We grabbed our stuff and the car and drove in silence to the cabin from before. The sun was dipping below the tree line, casting the forest in long shadows of purple and bruised orange. Inside, the cabin was dim, lit only by the hearth. The air smelled of woodsmoke and damp earth. It was small. It was safe.

I dropped my jacket on the hook by the door, the leather heavy with the weight of the day. Andre did the same. We moved around each other with a new, fragile rhythm. The violence of the last couple of hours; the ambush, the fight, the knife sliding into the Leader's chest, hung between us like smoke.

Andre stopped in the center of the room. He looked at his hands, then at mine.

"We need to get it off," he said, his voice raspy.

"The river water didn't work," I whispered.

"I know. We need hot water. Soap."

He walked to the small bathroom, the floorboards creaking under his boots. I followed. The bathroom was cramped, a shower stall with a cracked tile floor and a rusted drain. He turned the faucet handles, and the pipes groaned, but then the water came, steaming and hissing. He undressed first. His movements were slow, mechanical. When his shirt came off, I saw the blood, splattered across his shoulder and side, a dark arterial spray that had soaked into the fabric. He kicked off his boots and stepped into the stall. He didn't close the curtain. He held out a hand to me.

"Freya."

I took it. I stepped in with him. The stall was tight, forcing us flush against each other. The steam instantly fogged up the glass, wrapping us in a white haze. I stripped off my clothes, letting them fall to the wet floor. I didn't feel shy. I didn't feel the shame of the cult's teachings about the body being sinful. I just felt the need to be clean.

He pulled the chain on the shower head. The water rained down. We stood under the spray together. For a long time, we just let it hit us. I watched the water turn pink as it ran over his shoulder, swirling down the drain at our feet. It was the Leader washing away, leaving us.

Andre picked up a bar of soap. It was cheap, smelling of lemon, but it was all we had. He lathered his hands and then reached for mine. He washed me. It wasn't sexual. It was a reverent act. He scrubbed my palms, where the blood was stuck. He cleaned my knuckles, which were raw from the fight with the women. His hands were rough, calloused, but his touch was agonizingly gentle. I watched his face. He was focused, his brow furrowed, like he was trying to scrub away the sin that wasn't on his skin, but was staining his soul.

"Your hair," he said softly.

I turned my back to him. He worked the soap into my matted, tangled curls, his fingers massaging my scalp. It felt like a benediction. The tension of the day, the nightmares of the hypnosis, the screaming of the compound; it all sluiced off down the drain with the dirt and the blood.

I turned back around and took the soap from him.

"My turn," I said.

I washed his chest. The water ran red and pink over his muscles, tracing the lines of the scars he already had. I washed the blood of the man who had tried to own me. I traced the brand on his shoulder, the mark of the Enforcer he had been. He winced slightly as I washed around the wound. He watched me. His eyes were dark, his jaw tight. He wasn't looking at my body. He was looking at my face.

"You don't look at me like I'm a monster," he whispered, rinsing the soap off his skin.

"You're not a monster," I said. I reached up and washed the side of his neck, feeling his pulse hammering against my fingertips. "You're Andre."

He let out a breath that sounded like a sob, but he didn't cry. He leaned down, resting his forehead against mine. We stood there, entwined under the hot water, just breathing.

Eventually, the water ran clear. We got out and toweled off in the small room, sharing the single rough towel. I dressed in sweatpants and one of his t-shirts. It was too big, smelling of him and the lemon soap. It was the most comfortable thing I had ever worn.

I grabbed Andre's hand.

"What are you doing?" he rumbled.

"Fixing you," I said.

"I don't need fixing," he replied.

"Everyone needs fixing," I told him. "I see you, Andre. Even when you try to hide it."

He brought my fingers to his lips, kissing my knuckles.

"I see you too, Freya," he said, his voice dropping to that register that vibrated through my bones. "I see the wolf."

"I'm not a wolf," I whispered. "I'm just tired."

"You're alive," he corrected. "That's enough."

The day; the blood, the killing, the running, was over. In this small room, wearing his shirt, smelling of lemon and woodsmoke, I wasn't Freya the runaway, and he wasn't Andre the Enforcer. We were just two broken people stubborn enough to build a home out of the wreckage.

"I'll need to stitch that," I said, looking at the jagged tear in his shoulder where the bullet had gone through. "The bleeding stopped, but it's too wide to heal on its own."

Andre looked down at his shoulder, then at the needle and thread I'd found in the first aid kit. He frowned.

"You don't have to," he said, his voice rough.

"I want to. Now sit down."

He hesitated, then sat on the edge of the toilet lid. I positioned myself between his legs, kneeling on the bathmat to get to the right height. I cleaned the wound with an alcohol wipe. His hiss of breath was the only sound in the small room. The exit wound was ugly, a tear in the skin that looked like a second mouth.

"This will hurt," I warned, tearing the sterilising packet for the curved needle.

"Do it," he said, his eyes closing as he braced his hands on his knees.

I took a deep breath, my own hands shaking, and pushed the needle through the toughened skin. His muscle jumped under my touch, a reflex he couldn't control. He didn't make a sound, just gripped his knees tighter. I worked quickly, tying off the knots, the black thread biting into the flushed skin. It wasn't pretty. It was crude, ugly work, but I didn't stop until the flesh was pulled together. I leaned back and wiped the blood from my thumb.

"All done," I whispered.

He opened his eyes, looking down at the black X on his shoulder, then up at me.

"Thank you," he said.

I reached up and brushed the hair off his forehead.

"It's just stitches, Andre."

"No," he said, catching my hand. "It's you."

The gravity in his voice pulled the air out of the room. I sat back on my heels, looking up at him, and realised that while he was the one who had been shot, he was the one holding me together.

"We should get food," Andre said.

His voice was hoarse, scraped raw. I nodded, drifting toward the small kitchenette.

"We have... beans. Rice." I opened the cupboard. The shelves were bare except for a few tins and bags of dried goods. It wasn't much. It wasn't the bounty of the compound.

"We'll go shopping tomorrow," Andre said, coming up behind me. I turned to look at him. Up close, the smell of blood was fainter, masked by pine and the scent of him; leather, gun oil, sweat and now lemon too.

"Okay," I said.

He didn't move away immediately. He stood there, his body heat radiating against my back, surrounding me. I leaned forward, just an inch, letting myself rest against him.

"What?" he murmured.

"Nothing," I said. "Just... quiet."

It was domestic. It was terrifyingly normal. We were standing in a kitchen, talking about dinner, instead of running for our lives or killing a man. The contrast made my chest ache.

He stepped back, and I missed the warmth instantly.

"Fire," he said. "I'll start the fire." He moved to the stone hearth.

He built a fire while I braided my wet hair. I watched him crouch, arranging the logs with hands that had held a gun less than an hour ago. He didn't look like a monster now. He looked like a man providing for his home.

Home. The word settled over me, heavy and strange.

We cooked cans of beans and fried sliced potatoes in a cast iron skillet, then sat on the rug in front of the fireplace, the fire crackling, filling the room with warmth. I took a large bite. It was hot, it was plain, and for the first time since I met him, Andre laughed. It started as a small huff of breath as I struggled to get a potato with my fork. Then it grew, a low rumbling sound that vibrated through his chest. It was a beautiful sound, unguarded and real.

"What?" I asked, smiling around my fork.

"You're a mess," he said, grinning. He reached

out and wiped a smear of bean juice off my chin with his thumb. "It's everywhere."

"It's good to be messy," I said.

The laughter faded, but the ease remained.

"It's good," Andre said. He looked surprised.

"It's... just beans," I said.

"Tastes better than silence," he said.

He looked at me then, really looked at me. The firelight caught the sharp angles of his face, the hard line of his jaw, the darkness of his eyes. In this light, he wasn't the Enforcer. He was just Andre. He took a bite, chewing slowly.

"My mother would have liked it."

"Yeah?" I asked softly.

"She liked simple things," he said, staring into the fire. "Before the compound. She used to make toast. Burnt it mostly. But she was proud of it."

"She must have been hungry a lot," I said.

"Starving," he corrected. "It makes you appreciate a full belly."

He finished his bowl and set it down. He leaned back on his hands, looking at the ceiling. The fatigue was catching up with him. I saw the shadows under his eyes, the slump in his shoulders.

"Andre?"

"Hmm?"

"Are you... are you okay?"

He dropped his gaze to mine. He huffed a short, dark laugh.

"I just helped kill my father figure. I burned my life to the ground. I'm far from okay, Freya."

"I know," I said. "I just meant... here. With me."

The silence stretched, filled only by the crackle of the fire. He shifted, turning his body toward me.

"Yeah," he whispered. "I'm okay here." He reached out, his hand hovering over my knee. He didn't touch me, just let the heat of his skin bleed into my jeans. "I don't know what this is," he admitted. "This cabin. Us. It feels like a dream I'm not supposed to wake up from."

"Then don't wake up," I said.

I moved my hand, covering his. I pressed his palm against my leg, anchoring him. His fingers curled, interlocking with mine. His skin was rough, calloused, but the grip was gentle.

"I love you, Freya. I think I've loved you since I first laid eyes on you and saw that you weren't just a broken bird, but a phoenix ready to be reborn," he confessed.

I breathed in deeply, searching his gaze for the lie, the trick. But there was none. My smile bloomed, stretching from ear to ear.

"I love you, Andre. You were sent to break me. But instead, you fixed me."

We sat there, looking at the fire. The little bird and the Enforcer. The victim and the guard. The lines were blurring.

Later, when the fire had died to glowing embers, Andre moved to sit against the cabin wall, his long legs stretched out. I crawled over to him. It was comfortable. It was safe. But underneath the comfort was a jagged shard of fear. Fear that this couldn't last, that the son would find us, that the outside world would chew us up.

****

The nightmares came that night. I woke up to the sound of a shout. It wasn't me. It was Andre. I rolled over in bed. The cabin was dark, moonlight leaking through the curtains. Andre was thrashing on the floor beside the bed, his legs tangled in the sheets, sweat pouring down his face.

"No!" he gasped, his voice breaking. "Don't take her! Don't!"

He was fighting. Fighting a ghost.

"Andre!"

I scrambled out of bed, dropping to my knees beside him. The floorboards were cold, biting into my skin. I grabbed his shoulders, trying to pin him down without hurting him.

"Andre, wake up!"

His eyes flew open. They were wild, unseeing, full of a terror so deep it made my breath hitch. He lunged up, throwing me off balance, his hands locking around my throat. I gasped, my hands flying to his wrists, but he didn't squeeze. He just held me there, his thumbs pressing against my pulse point.

"It's me," I choked out. "It's Freya. You're

safe."

He froze. The wildness in his eyes fractured. The reality of the room bled in; dark wood, moonlight, the smell of pine. He looked at his hands around my neck, looked at my face, and the realisation hit him like a physical blow. He let go like I'd burned him, scrambling backward until his back hit the bed frame. He buried his face in his hands, his shoulders shaking.

"I'm sorry," he rasped, his voice muffled. "I'm sorry."

"It's okay," I said, scooting closer to him. I hesitated, then reached out to touch his chest. His muscles were bunched tight as rocks. "It was just a dream."

He shook his head.

"No. It wasn't." He looked up, his eyes red-rimmed. "She was there. My mother. She was standing there... in the blood. She was crying. She said I betrayed her. She said I'm killing her."

My heart broke for him. It cracked open, the way the riverbank had cracked for me. I had seen his strength, his violence, his dominance. I had never seen his scars.

"She wouldn't leave him," he said, his voice hollow. "Not even for me. That's how deep it goes."

He looked down at his hands, turning them over, staring at his palms like they were foreign objects. He was broken. The Enforcer was gone, leaving just a man who had broken his mother's heart.

I moved closer, sitting cross-legged beside him. I didn't ask permission. I just did it.

"She's not dead, Andre," I said firmly. "And she's not gone. She's just... trapped. Like I was."

He looked at me, his eyes glistening with unshed tears.

"I freed you."

"And now I'm freeing you," I said. I reached out and took one of his hands. His fingers were ice cold. I brought it to my face, pressing his palm against my cheek. He flinched, his breath catching. "I see your scars," I whispered. "I see them, Andre. Even the ones you can't show me."

His gaze dropped to my neck, where his hands had been moments before. He swallowed hard.

"I'm sorry I hurt you."

"You didn't," I said. "You saved me. And now... let me save you." I moved his hand, placing it over my heart. "Feel that?"

He stared at me, his eyes searching mine.

"It's racing," he said.

"That's because we're alive," I said. "That's because we're here."

He leaned forward slowly, resting his forehead against mine. It was a surrender, but not in submission. In trust. We sat there in the dark, wrapped in each other, while the moonlight painted us in silver. The cabin was small, but the world inside it was vast. We weren't captor and captive anymore. We weren't running and chasing. We were two broken people leaning on each other so we wouldn't fall.

CHAPTER 31

Freya

The death of a man does not always mean the death of the idea. We had fled the compound with blood on our hands and the Leader's son's threats ringing in our ears, but the world didn't end. The sky didn't crack open. For weeks, there was only the endless grey ribbon of the highway and the heavy silence between us, punctuated only by the occasional hiss of pain from Andre as he leaned against the car door, clutching his wounded shoulder.

We didn't go back to the city. We didn't disappear into a crowd. We found a small town tucked into the folds of the mountains, far enough from the compound that the air felt different, but close enough to the trees that the scent of pine still triggered a flare of panic in my chest. It was a reprieve. That was all. We didn't destroy the cult entirely. As the Leader fell, his son stepped into the breach, groomed for succession since birth. I had seen the look in his eyes as we ran; cold, devoid of grief, burning with a righteous, terrifying purpose. He was marshaling the survivors who remained loyal, the ones who were too far gone to see the bars of their own cage. What should have been victory was a mere pause in a war that had only changed shape.

We rented a small house at the end of a dirt road. It had a porch that sagged in the middle and a kitchen that smelled of old dust and lemon cleaner. It was the first place I had ever lived that didn't have a schedule taped to the fridge. We were trying to learn how to be people instead of weapons and prey.

The first few weeks were a strange, fragile hallucination of normalcy. We went to the grocery store, a mundane miracle that left me shaking in the cereal aisle. I stood there for twenty minutes, staring at the colourful boxes, overwhelmed by the sheer volume of choice. No one told me what to buy. No one watched my hands. Andre found me there. He didn't rush me. He just stood at the end of the aisle, his large hands resting loosely in the pockets of his jeans, watching the exit with a predator's stillness.

"Take your time, Freya," he'd said when I finally looked at him, my eyes stinging.

We walked the quiet streets of the town, hand in hand. I waited for the shame to come, the shame of holding hands with the man who had hunted me, the man who had tied me up and dragged me back to hell. But it didn't come. We were fully committed to each other now, lovers who had chosen to turn our brokenness into a shared language instead of a sentence.

But trauma is a ghost that lives under the skin. At night, the cabin felt smaller. The darkness brought the nightmares back. I would wake up gasping, the bright white lights of the Leader's interrogation room flashing behind my eyelids. I would hear the chanting; You will become one with us all, until the walls of the bedroom seemed to breathe. Andre would hold me through it. His arms were the only anchor that kept me from drifting away into madness. He would whisper to me in the dark, his voice a low rumble against my ear, telling me I was safe, that I was real. But I knew he was fighting his own ghosts.

He never talked about his mother again. He didn't have to. I saw it in the way he flinched when a phone rang, expecting it to be the Leader. The way his eyes went distant when he saw a woman with grey hair in the grocery store. He felt her hatred like a brand. He had sedated her to save her life, and in her eyes, he was the devil. He had betrayed his father figure and his mother in the same stroke. The guilt was a heavy cloak he wore, one I couldn't quite lift from his shoulders, no matter how hard I tried.

Yet, in the quiet moments, we found a way to breathe. I stood by the stove one evening, stirring a pot of soup. The steam curled up, fogging the window. Andre came up behind me, wrapping his arms around my waist, burying his face in my neck. He was careful of his shoulder, still healing, but his presence was overwhelming, a solid wall of heat at my back.

"Dinner's almost ready," I whispered.

He hummed against my skin, the vibration travelling down my spine. He pressed a kiss to the sensitive spot just below my ear.

"My fierce little bird," he murmured.

Once, the name had been a taunt. It had been a reminder that I was small, fragile, something to be caged. Now, his voice curled around the words with a tenderness that made my chest ache. He called me little bird not because I was weak, but because I had flown when he tried to clip my wings. I had risen like a phoenix instead of being a caged canary.

I leaned back into him, closing my eyes.

"I hate that nickname," I lied softly.

"Liar," he said, and I could hear the smile in his voice.

He was right. I hated myself a little less each time I realised I liked it.

But we never stopped training. We weren't just hiding. We were preparing. Every day, in the clearing behind the cabin, Andre taught me how to fight. Not just how to escape, but how to strike, how to disable, how to wound. We were intent on helping those still left at the compound. We knew we had to go back. We knew the war wasn't over.

The illusion held for three months. It shattered on a Tuesday morning. I was in the living room, dusting the bookshelf; a mindless task that I found strangely soothing, when I heard a sound on the porch. Not a knock. A soft thud. Like something heavy being set down.

I froze, the rag clutched in my hand.

"Andre?"

He was in the kitchen, sharpening his knife. The sound of the stone against steel stopped instantly. He was at my side in a second, his body shifting from relaxed lover to Enforcer in a heartbeat.

"Stay behind me," he ordered.

He moved to the door, his gun drawn. I held my breath, my heart hammering a frantic rhythm against my ribs. I expected to see the son's face. I expected to see a squad of guards with rifles raised. But the porch was empty. The morning sun slanted across the wood, illuminating a small, brown package wrapped in twine. It sat in the center of the welcome mat.

Andre scanned the tree line, his eyes sharp, searching for movement. Seeing nothing, he holstered his gun and bent down. He picked up the package. It looked light. He brought it inside and placed it on the kitchen table. We both stared at it as if it were a bomb.

"Open it," I whispered.

Andre cut the twine with the knife he had been sharpening. He peeled back the brown paper. There was no note. No letter. Just two pieces of jewellery resting on a bed of white cotton. My necklace. The silver compass with four points. Loyalty, Perfection, Worship, Truth. And next to it, a thick silver bracelet. Andre's bracelet. It bore the same symbol. Both were tarnished, but the engraving was deep, unmistakable. The brand of the cult.

"He's found us," I said, the blood draining from my face.

Andre picked up the bracelet. His hand was steady, but I saw the muscle jump in his jaw.

"The son."

The message was clear, more terrifying than any letter could have been. You do not outrun a past you have not yet burned. He knew where we slept. He knew who we were. He was reminding us that we were still marked. That no matter how far we ran, or how much we pretended to be normal people in a small town, we belonged to them.

I looked at the necklace. I remembered the day it was put around my neck. I remembered the way it had felt like a collar.

"He wants us to come back," Andre said, his voice low and dangerous. "He's making a statement."

"He's telling us we can't hide."

Andre looked at me, his eyes dark with a fierce, possessive light. He reached out, taking my hand.

"We're not going back as captives, Freya."

"No," I said, my voice trembling but gaining strength. "We're not."

The man who once hunted me and I stood together in the doorway of our latest refuge, the metal symbols glinting in our palms. We looked out at the quiet street, the innocent trees. We knew we were still marked. We had killed a leader, but we had not killed the ideology that shaped us. The rot ran deep. The danger curled around our love like smoke, choking and dark.

The illusion was over.

Andre squeezed my hand, his grip tight enough to hurt, grounding me.

"Ready?"

I looked at him; at the wound on his shoulder, the lines of strain around his eyes, the steely determination that had saved my life. I realised then that I wasn't afraid of the son. I wasn't afraid of the fight. I was only afraid of losing this. Of losing the language we had built from the wreckage.

"Ready," I said.

We turned away from the safety of the cabin, leaving the necklace and the bracelet on the table. We didn't need the symbols to know who we were anymore. We were on the move again, hand in hand, walking toward the car, away from the life we had tried to build. We were leaving the sanctuary behind, determined to rewrite control into choice even if the world insisted on chaining us to what we were. Our river of escape had turned red, slick with blood and sacrifice. But we walked forward, not as victim and enforcer, but as two broken people stubborn enough to build something fierce and honest out of the wreckage.

The hunt was on. And this time, we were the hunters too.

EPILOGUE

Julian

Julian stood in the center of the room, feeling the weight of the silence press against him. He felt no grief. He felt... light. The burden of leadership, the crown, the thousands of eyes waiting for direction, was gone. In its place was a cold, sharp focus. He looked down at his father. The old man looked smaller without breathing. The veneer of the holy father had evaporated, leaving behind a pathetic shell of flesh. Julian felt no urge to weep. He felt only ruthless clarity. The cult was a machine, and the machine had stuttered. He was the mechanic now. He would fix it.

A groan from the couch made him turn. Cynthia's eyes fluttered. They were glazed, dilated from the drugs, but slowly, intelligence returned to them. Confusion washed over her face, followed by a dawning horror.

"Julian?" He didn't look at her. He walked to the sideboard, pulling the curtains open. The sun was beginning to bleed into the room, harsh and unyielding. "Is the Leader..."

Cynthia struggled to sit up, clutching at the blanket he had used to cover her legs. Her voice was a wreck. "Is he... gone?"

"He has ascended," Julian said.

His voice was perfectly level, a calm that was more terrifying than tears. Cynthia froze. The blood drained from her face, leaving her pale and gaunt.

"Ascended?"

"He has left his vessel," Julian said, turning to face her. He took her by the arm, his grip firm but not cruel. He pulled her to her feet. "We must be strong, Cynthia. We cannot show them we are lost. We are not lost."

She stared at him, her eyes darting between his face and the empty body on the floor. The structure of her reality was collapsing.

"But... What happened to Andre?" she stammered, the name sticking in her throat like a sob.

"He is a traitor," Julian said, the judgment final. "He has taken the girl. He has turned his back on his promise. He is infected."

"He is my son!" she cried out, pushing against his chest, her fists weak. "He wouldn't."

"He is a soldier who broke," Julian said, pushing her back gently but firmly. He guided her toward the door. "Come. We must clean up this mess. The Father... he wouldn't want to see it like this."

He opened the door. The entire compound was silent. The air was thick with the scent of burning wood and fear. Julian stepped out onto the porch. He looked down at the women gathered there. They looked lost. Without the Leader's voice, they were like sheep without a shepherd. They looked at Julian, their eyes wide and pleading, waiting for him to speak first.

"Go to the prayer hall," Julian commanded. "Cynthia, lead them. Pray. Cleanse. Show them we are not afraid. We are one with us all."

Cynthia nodded slowly. She wiped her face, straightened her back, and began to walk toward the great hall. The women followed her like ducklings.

Julian watched them go, then turned to one of the Enforcers; a heavy-set man named Thomas.

"Thomas."

"Sir?"

"Take a car," Julian said. "Find where the Enforcer and the traitor are staying. Use the tracker."

Thomas looked at the map, then at Julian, suspicion warring in his eyes.

"Sir?"

"Take this," Julian ordered, his eyes hard. He handed over a package wrapped in brown paper and tied with twine. "Leave it on their doorstep. I want them to know we are coming."

Thomas nodded slowly, understanding. The message was simple. A scare tactic, a psychological blow designed to make them look over their shoulders. It meant: I see you, you are marked, and you are mine. And it was the start of the game.

He wasn't driven by grief. He was driven by a cold, pragmatic instinct. He would be the father this place needed. He would hunt the traitor and the girl. He would burn the rot away.

Julian smiled. It wasn't a warm smile. It was the smile of a predator who knows the trap has been baited and the jaws were about to snap.

The cat was in the mousehole. And the mouse didn't even know.

AUTHOR'S NOTE

This story was born from my obsession with H.D. Carlton's Haunting Adeline and Hunting Adeline. Her work inspired me to chase the kind of writing that crawls under your skin and refuses to leave; the kind that makes you question everything while simultaneously craving more. While I've never experienced the darkness of cults or the specific horrors within these pages, I do understand what it feels like to be pulled from suffocation into freedom. That moment when you finally breathe; really breathe, and realise you're alive. That feeling runs through every word of this book.

My hope for you, dear reader, is that you finish this book stunned. Emotionally invested. Caught in that thrilling, unsettling blend of fear and desire that only dark romance can deliver. I want you to feel everything; the ugly, the beautiful, the unforgivable. Book two is coming, and I'm beyond excited for the emotional journey these characters will take us on. We're not done yet, not even close. Thank you for stepping into the cage with me.

ACKNOWLEDGE-MENTS

To my Beta and ARC readers, thank you for taking a chance on this book before anyone else. Your feedback, your enthusiasm, and your willingness to dive into the darkness with me means everything.

To Aunty Joy, you were the first to read this story and give me real, honest feedback. Thank you for your time, your insight, and for believing this book was worth finishing. Your support means the world.

To Natalie, thank you for being my constant supporter through life. Your belief in me, even when I didn't believe in myself, has carried me through more than you know. I'm so grateful to have you.

And to every reader who picked up this book; you're the reason I write. Thank you for your courage, your curiosity, and your hunger for stories that don't hold back.

Thank you for reading A Cage Painted Red.
Freya and Andre's story continues...

SNEAK PEEK - A COMPASS STAINED BLACK

CHAPTER 1

Freya

The highway stretched ahead like a promise we couldn't keep. Andre's hands gripped the steering wheel with the kind of tension that made his knuckles go white. His left shoulder was still bandaged beneath his jacket, the wound from our escape three months old but still tender. Every time he shifted gears, I saw him wince; a tiny fracture in the armor he wore for my benefit.

I stared at the burner phone in my lap. It was cheap, plastic, anonymous. The kind of phone you bought when you were planning to disappear. The FBI's hotline number was already punched in, waiting for me to hit the green button.

One call. That's all it would take.

"Don't," Andre said, his voice low and rough. He didn't look at me. He kept his eyes on the road, scanning the rearview mirror like Julian's men would materialise out of the darkness at any moment.

"I didn't say anything," I replied.

"You don't have to. I can hear you thinking."

I turned the phone over in my hands. The screen glowed faintly in the dim interior of the car. Outside, the landscape was nothing but shadow and the occasional flicker of distant farmhouse lights. We'd been driving for six hours straight, heading north with no real destination. Just away. Always away.

"If we go to the FBI," I started.

"We lose control," Andre finished. His jaw was set, that sharp line of stubbornness I'd come to recognise. "The second we hand this over to them, it becomes their story. Their narrative. Their timeline."

"And Julian wins," I whispered.

"Julian wins," he confirmed.

I pressed the power button and watched the screen go dark. The phone felt heavier now, useless and damning all at once. I shoved it into the glove compartment and slammed it shut.

Andre's hand found mine across the center console. His palm was warm, calloused, steady. He squeezed once.

"We'll figure it out," he said.

I wanted to believe him. I wanted to believe we could outrun a ghost, that we could dismantle an empire built on devotion and fear with nothing but our anger and a stolen car. But the memory of that package on our doorstep still haunted me; the brown paper, the twine, the necklace and bracelet inside. Our old symbols. Our old chains.

Julian knew where we'd been sleeping. He knew what we'd tried to build in that cabin with the sagging porch and the smell of lemon cleaner. He knew, and he wanted us to know he knew.

The message was clear: You cannot outrun what you are.

"There," Andre said, nodding toward a flickering neon sign up ahead. MOTEL. VACANCY. The letters buzzed and blinked, half of them burned out. It looked like the kind of place where people paid in cash and didn't ask questions.

Perfect.

Andre pulled into the gravel lot, parking the car in the shadows away from the main office. He killed the engine, and the silence rushed in like a flood. For a moment, we just sat there, listening to the tick of the cooling engine and the distant hum of the highway.

"One night," I said.

"One night," Andre agreed. "Then we move again."

He got out first, scanning the lot with the practiced eye of a man who'd spent years hunting people like us. Satisfied, he came around to my side and opened the door. I stepped out into the cold night air, pulling my jacket tighter around me.

The motel office smelled like cigarettes and old coffee. A man sat behind the counter, his face illuminated by the blue glow of a television playing some late-night talk show. He barely looked up when we walked in.

"Room for the night," Andre said, sliding two twenties across the counter.

The man grunted, took the cash, and handed over a key attached to a plastic tag with a faded number 7. "Check out's at ten. No refunds."

"Understood."

We walked back out into the night. Room 7 was at the far end of the building, tucked away from the parking lot lights. Andre unlocked the door, and I stepped inside.

The room was exactly what I expected: a double bed with a worn floral comforter, a television bolted to the dresser, a bathroom with tiles that had probably been white once. It smelled faintly of bleach and something I didn't want to identify.

Andre locked the door behind us, sliding the chain into place. Then he pulled the curtains closed, blocking out the neon glow from the sign outside. In the dim light of the single bedside lamp, he looked older than his years; exhausted, haunted, still every inch the Enforcer he'd been trained to be.

"Get some sleep," he said, moving to check the bathroom, the closet, anywhere someone might hide.

"You need to sleep too," I countered. "Your shoulder—"

"Is fine."

"Andre—"

He turned to face me, and the look in his eyes stopped me cold. It was the look of a man who'd been hunted before, who knew the cost of letting his guard down even for a second.

"I'll sleep when I know we're safe," he said quietly. "Right now, I need to make sure no one followed us."

I wanted to argue. I wanted to tell him I could keep watch, that he didn't have to carry the weight of my survival on his damaged shoulder. But the truth was, I was exhausted. Bone-deep, soul-tired exhausted. The kind of tired that made my hands shake and my thoughts blur.

So I nodded. I kicked off my shoes and climbed onto the bed, pulling the thin comforter over me. It smelled like industrial detergent and other people's sleep.

Andre sat in the chair by the window, positioning himself so he could see both the door and the parking lot through a gap in the curtains. He pulled his gun from his waistband and set it on the small table beside him.

"Andre?" I said into the darkness.

"Yeah?"

"Do you think we can actually do this? Take down Julian? Free the others?"

He was quiet for a long moment. Then: "I think we have to try."

It wasn't the answer I wanted, but it was the

truth. And right now, truth was the only thing we had left.

I woke to Andre's hand over my mouth.

My eyes flew open, panic spiking through my chest. But Andre's face was inches from mine, his expression calm but urgent. He put a finger to his lips.

Quiet.

He removed his hand slowly, and that's when I heard it. Footsteps. Outside the door. Slow, deliberate. Someone checking the room numbers.

Andre was already moving, gun in hand, positioning himself beside the door. He motioned for me to get into the bathroom. I slid off the bed as quietly as I could, my heart hammering so loud I was sure whoever was outside could hear it.

The footsteps stopped. Right outside our door.

A shadow passed across the gap under the door. Then another. Two people, at least.

I pressed myself against the bathroom doorframe, watching Andre. His body was coiled, ready to spring. Every muscle tense. This was the man who'd hunted runaways for years. The predator, not the prey.

A knock. Three sharp raps that made my breath catch.

"Housekeeping," a voice called. Female, bored, completely wrong for 3 AM.

Andre didn't move. Didn't respond.

Another knock. "Housekeeping. Need to check the smoke detector."

I saw Andre's jaw tighten. It was a terrible lie. No one checked smoke detectors at three in the morning.

The doorknob rattled. Someone was trying to open it.

Andre raised his gun, aimed at chest height.

The rattling stopped. Footsteps retreated down the walkway. Voices, low and male, conferring. Then the sound of car doors opening and closing. An engine starting.

We waited in the darkness, not moving, barely breathing. Minutes crawled by. Finally, Andre moved to the window and peered through the curtains.

"They're gone," he said, but his voice was tight. "For now."

"How?" I breathed. "Andre, how did they find us again?"

He turned to look at me, and I saw the same question burning in his eyes. The same fear that was clawing its way up my throat.

"I swept the car for tracking devices before we left the cabin," he said. "There was nothing. I checked our clothes, our bags. We left everything behind that could have been compromised."

"Then how?" My voice was rising, panic bleeding through. "We've been on the road for hours. We paid cash. We didn't tell anyone where we were going. We didn't even know where we were going."

Andre holstered his gun and moved to me, his hands gripping my shoulders. "I don't know. But we need to leave. Now."

We threw our few belongings into the duffel bag; clothes we'd bought at a gas station, toiletries, nothing that connected us to our old lives. Andre checked the parking lot one more time before we slipped out the door.

The car was where we'd left it, untouched. Andre did another sweep anyway, checking under the hood, under the chassis, in the wheel wells. Nothing.

"Get in," he said.

We drove through the night with no destination, Andre constantly checking the rearview mirror, taking random turns, doubling back. Professional countersurveillance tactics.

"Twice," I said as dawn started to break over the horizon. "They've found us twice now."

"The cabin I understand," Andre said, his jaw tight. "We were there three months. Got comfortable. Someone in town could have recognised us, made a call."

"But this?" I gestured back toward the motel we'd fled. "We were there for a few hours, Andre. In the middle of nowhere. We paid cash. How could they possibly—"

"I don't know," he cut me off, and I could hear the frustration bleeding through his careful control. "Maybe they have eyes everywhere. Maybe

Julian has more resources than we thought."

I wanted to push, to demand answers neither of us had. But the exhaustion was setting in, making my thoughts fuzzy.

"We need to move faster," I finally said. "Never stay anywhere more than a night. Keep moving."

"Agreed."

Andre pulled off onto a side road and parked. He turned to face me, his expression serious.

"Listen to me," he said. "We're going to figure this out. There's a logical explanation. There has to be. We just need to be smarter."

"We've been smart," I said, my voice breaking. "We've done everything right."

"Then we need to be smarter than smart."

He pulled me against his chest, and I let myself collapse into him for just a moment. His heart beat steady and strong under my ear. Real. Solid. The only thing I was sure of anymore.

"What if we can never stop running?" I whispered.

"Then we run," Andre said simply. "But we run together. And eventually, Freya, we're going to turn around and make them run from us."

I pulled back to look at him. In the grey morning light, he looked dangerous. Not the kind of dangerous that Father Michael had been; cold and calculated and cruel. But the kind of dangerous that came from having nothing left to lose.

"Promise me something," I said.

"Anything."

"If they catch us. If Julian gets his hands on us again." I swallowed hard. "Don't let him take me back alive. Don't let him put me in another cage."

Andre's expression went dark. He cupped my face in his hands, his thumbs brushing away tears I didn't realise I'd shed.

"That's not going to happen," he said fiercely. "Do you hear me? I will burn down every compound, kill every enforcer, tear Julian apart with my bare hands before I let him touch you again."

"Promise me anyway."

For a long moment, he just looked at me. Then he leaned forward and pressed his forehead to mine.

"I promise," he whispered. "But it won't come to that. Because we're going to win."

I wanted to believe him. God, I wanted to believe him so badly it hurt.

Instead, I kissed him. Hard and desperate and clinging. Like if I held on tight enough, the world couldn't tear us apart.

When we finally broke apart, the sun was rising over the mountains, painting the sky in shades of red and gold. Beautiful and terrible all at once.

Andre started the car again.

"Where to?" I asked.

"West," he said. "Somewhere they won't

think to look."

As we pulled back onto the highway, I watched the sunrise in the rearview mirror. Red sky in the morning, sailors take warning.

Somewhere behind us, Julian was coming.

The hunt was on.

ABOUT THE AUTHOR

Jessica Nicholls

I'm an avid dark romance fan with a passion for stories that get your heart racing and your pulse pounding. Based in Tauranga, New Zealand, I spend my days chasing a very energetic three-year-old, devouring books that most people would call "unhinged," and eating far too much chocolate.

I love writing anything that makes you feel; whether that's fear, desire, rage, or that delicious discomfort that comes from morally grey characters making terrible decisions. If it's dark, twisted, and emotionally devastating, I'm here for it.

A Cage Painted Red is my debut novel in the dark romance space, though I did self-publish a semi-autobiographical fiction piece when I was sixteen for a school project (we don't talk about that one).

When I'm not writing, you can find me with my nose in a book, pretending I have my life together, or convincing my toddler that vegetables are, in fact, edible.

Made in the USA
Coppell, TX
29 June 2026

82449567R00194